Murder by Moonlight

FELINES OF FAIRYTALE FOREST
BOOK ONE

K. L. MONTGOMERY

Cover design by the author, made with images licensed through DepositPhotos.
Map created by Kadan Knapp.
Paperback ISBN: 978-1-949394-75-7

Published by Mountains Wanted Publishing
P.O. Box 50
Harbeson, DE 19951
mountainswanted.com

❀ Created with Vellum

When murder strikes at their amusement park, Cat and the Felines of Fairytale Forest must solve a roller coaster of a case!

At Fairytale Forest, a theme park in the South Carolina Lowcountry, the custodial staff and a clowder of feral cats keep things neat and tidy. Until something *very* messy happens—one of the custodial managers is found strangled to death.

Catherine Lyon is a night shift custodian who finds herself topping the list of suspects. Sure, no one liked the victim—but someone really hated her enough to murder her in cold blood on the main street of the park? Cat certainly didn't do it—and she wants to prove it by finding the *real* killer.

She's shocked when Zoe, a member of the cat colony charged with eliminating vermin in the park, leads her to the dead body and the first clue. Can Cat, Zoe and the rest of the felines clean up the mess and solve the murder of the manipulative, mean-spirited manager?

Murder by Moonlight is the first book in the Felines of Fairytale Forest cozy mystery series. Visit a southern amusement park full of fantasy creatures and feline exterminators and meet Cat, a tenacious fifty-something custodian, and her spirited coworker Gloria. These ladies just can't resist a good mystery. Follow the clues and solve the case alongside Cat, Gloria and the whole furry gang!

Fairytale Forest Map

CREDIT: KADAN KNAPP

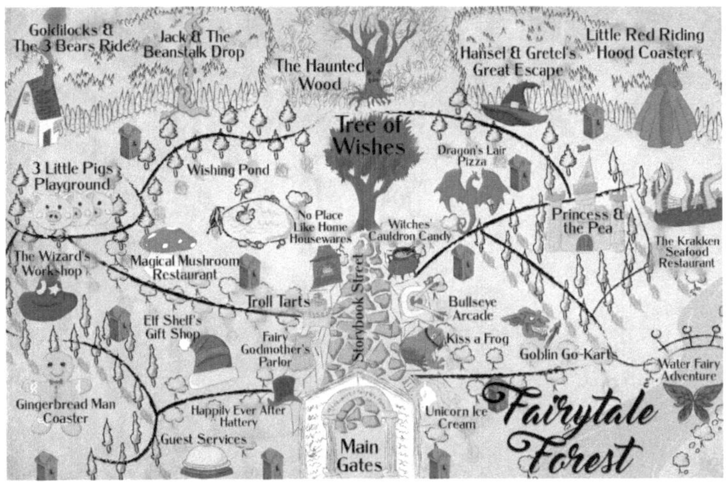

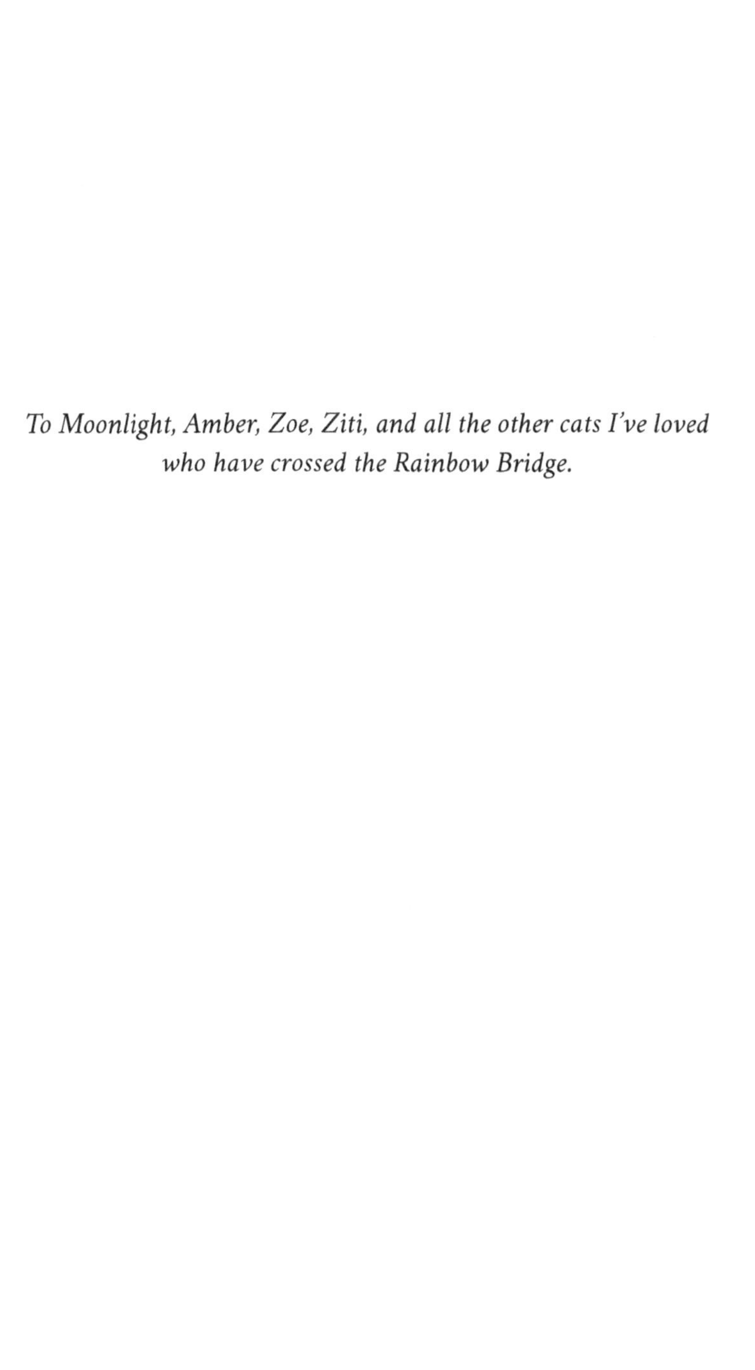

To Moonlight, Amber, Zoe, Ziti, and all the other cats I've loved who have crossed the Rainbow Bridge.

Gazing across the city of Charleston and the Ashley River, the shadowy figure adjusted the binoculars to focus on the target. The live oaks and pines were so thick, it was nearly impossible to see the structures that made up Fairytale Forest.

The theme park had been around for decades, but if the villain, driven by greed and revenge, had their way...Fairytale Forest's days were numbered.

And the perfect plan to close down the park was in the works.

One

CATHERINE

"Family traditions are cool and all, but this one is definitely *not* my favorite," Jayden Forest admitted as he pushed a broom down Storybook Street, the main thoroughfare in his family's theme park.

I cocked my head, the midnight breeze coming off the Ashley River rustling my hair. "Understood, but I admire your parents for keeping the tradition alive. Just think, your father stood right where you are when he was your age. He might've even been pushing the same broom!" I laughed as I pushed the rickety janitorial cart that likely dated back to the 1960s when Fairytale Forest first opened.

Jayden rolled his eyes. "You'd think they could spring for some new equipment at least."

"You know your parents—they not only believe in carrying on your grandparents' traditions, but 'waste not, want not' is their mantra. Along with 'if it ain't broke, don't fix it.'"

Jayden scanned the towering tree structure that stood at the end of Storybook Street. "I know. I guess I should just feel blessed I'll inherit this place someday. Well, me and my siblings."

"Your parents are in great health. It's going to be a long while before that happens!" I reminded him.

Jayden Forest was a phenomenal kid, though a little spoiled, being the baby of the family. But his parents were teaching him how to work for a living, and I didn't mind being a bit of a mentor to him. He wouldn't be working the custodial night shift for long. By next year, he'd be doing something more glamorous for sure.

I'd still be here, though. Pushing this same dang cart.

"How long have you worked here, Cat?" Jayden swept a small pile of leaves and trash into a dust pan.

I looked down at my hands momentarily, surveying the prominent veins that had just started to pop up in the last few years. My hands were starting to look like my mother's. I remembered them well.

"Let's see, I got this job almost twenty years ago. I'd just gotten divorced. I hadn't worked since before my kids were born, so I didn't have much of a resume. Your grandparents welcomed me on board with open arms."

"You never wanted to do anything else in the park?" Jayden's dark hair was ruffled by the wind, which had suddenly picked up.

"Nope." I pushed the cart along, heading for the restrooms at the corner of the courtyard that opened out on the centerpiece of Fairytale Forest, a lucky thirteen-story tree with a number of cables running above the canopy of pines and live oaks. The cables were part of an aerial tram system that transported visitors to various attractions at opposite corners of the park.

I sucked in the breeze floating off the river. "I like it here at night. It's quiet. Karen's not my favorite, but Walter is easy to work for, and I don't have to deal with too many people. I wouldn't want to be in the park in the daytime when it's too people-y."

The young man's head tipped back as laughter spilled out of his mouth. It felt good to entertain someone, but it was the truth. My longevity here and the cloak of night and quiet allowed me to do my best thinking. I wouldn't want to give that up. It brought peace to my soul.

"My dad said I would be here about six months before my next rotation begins," Jay explained. "But I can kind of see the draw." He stopped abruptly and frowned. "Except when I step in gum. Ugh."

"Occupational hazard," I quipped, grabbing the Goo Be Gone from the cart. I was armed and dangerous with this stuff.

It was just another night in paradise, otherwise known as after-hours in a family amusement park. As I helped Jayden scrape the gum off his shoe and the pavement, one of the park cats roamed out and stopped to watch us.

Jayden jumped a little then laughed. "I always forget we have cats here. I never see them during the day."

"It was your grandmother's idea, you know. A brilliant one at that. The cats keep the mice and other rodents away. I have never seen a mouse in all my years working in the park."

"That's amazing." He bent down and held out his hand to see if the cat would come over to him.

"You're not supposed to interact with them," I reminded him gently. "We aren't supposed to feed them or give them any attention so they don't become too accustomed to humans."

But Jayden was crouched down, beckoning the cat over to him. "But this one is so cute! What's its name?"

I looked at the fluffy feline with long gray fur. She glanced around and then casually began to lick her paw. We weren't supposed to interact with the cats, but we did have names for them. "That's Zoe. I am the one who got to name her. She just looks like a Zoe to me."

"Zoe. I like that. She's really pretty. Her fur is the same color as your hair," Jayden helpfully observed.

Sigh. Yeah, he didn't have to remind me that I'd gone completely gray in the past few years. Kids were good at pointing out stuff like that. Mine were all grown up and out of the house. The younger one just moved out last year. It was lonely living by myself, but I always looked forward to coming to work.

"Hey, did you clean the bathrooms yet?" my work bestie's bubbly voice cut through the humid night air.

"Hey yourself!" I shouted back at her, waiting for her to appear out of the shadows.

Gloria stepped out from behind the Witch's Cauldron candy store on the corner across from the restrooms. She'd wound a colorful scarf around her head, and her crown of salt-and-pepper braids sprang out from it like confetti. "We could clean it together? I'll take the men's, and you take the women's?"

I shook my head, onto her ploy. "You know as well as I do the women's restrooms are usually worse."

She laughed. "You got me there. Wanna do them together?"

"Fine." I smiled and turned to Jayden. "Finish sweeping the courtyard, and we'll meet you in the staff lounge in an hour for our break."

"Okay. Have fun, ladies." He dipped his chin and swept his way toward the enormous tree.

Zoe scampered off into the bushes, and I heard a slight scuffle. She either found prey to chase, or she was asserting herself. The feral cats were known to have tiffs here and there, and Zoe was one of the dominant ones. She led the small band of cats that hung out in the bushes surrounding the central courtyard.

I followed Gloria into the women's restroom. Paper towels littered the floor, and one of the toilets was overflowing.

"Oh my word!" Gloria exclaimed, her hands immediately flying to cover her nose. "Good gracious, it stinks to high heavens in here."

"Might need to call Chuck in Maintenance for that last stall." I pointed to where the water was leaking out onto the concrete floor. "Let's do that and start in the men's instead."

"Good plan." She nodded as I whipped out my walkie-talkie and put in a call to Maintenance.

The men's restroom was less of a disaster. We talked as we scrubbed everything down. It made the time and unpleasant tasks go faster.

"Did you hear about Heather's latest?" Gloria asked as she sprayed down the sinks and wiped the mirrors.

"What is that awful woman up to now?" I rolled my eyes. Heather Suka was the day-shift custodial supervisor, and no one liked her. Actually, that was putting it mildly. I couldn't think of a single person at Fairytale Forest who didn't loathe her.

"Someone said she and Walter were caught messing around out behind the Guest Services building!" The rumor exploded out of Gloria's mouth like she'd been holding it in all night.

I gasped. "What?! Walter wouldn't do that! He's happily married." Walter McDuff was in charge of custodial services in the entire park. I didn't care much for Karen York, our immediate supervisor, so I always went to Walter when I had an issue, and he never let me down.

Gloria shrugged. "Well, it's what I heard, anyway. I didn't believe it either, but I'm sure as heck not gonna let that one go by without comment."

"Well, no." When I joined in her laughter, the sound bounced all around the cement walls of the restroom, likely echoing into the park.

Seconds later, footsteps sounded on the concrete floor. "Are you two working in here or having comedy hour?" snarled a familiar voice. That grating, nasal Midwestern accent could only belong to Karen, our immediate supervisor.

She wasn't as hated as Heather, but she did live up to her name.

"Comedy hour," Gloria deadpanned, her fists flying to her hips. She cocked her head. "Don't worry. Our whole routine is about how men can't hit the toilet, but they sure love shooting things. Maybe if we made it into a video game?"

A slight smirk cracked Karen's pasty-white face. "Heather's called a meeting at six AM when she and day shift come in. Make sure you're there."

"But we're supposed to clock out at six," I complained.

"I'll see you at six," Karen reiterated, and then she

stomped right on out of the restroom, her footsteps pounding into the concrete and echoing off the walls as she went.

Gloria rolled her eyes. "Naked mud wrestling—who ya got, Heather or Karen?"

"Eww. Does it have to be naked?" I grimaced. "But definitely Heather. You just know she'd play dirty. Pardon the pun."

My work bestie threw her head back as laughter spilled out of her mouth. "Agreed. Karen is always by-the-book. And always brown-nosing Walter. She'd probably lick his boots if he let her."

We both had a good laugh thinking about the two shift supervisors going head-to-head in a mud-filled pit. They didn't exactly get along, what with both of them having extremely abrasive personalities.

That laugh would hopefully carry us right through till it was time to clock out in the morning.

ZOE

IF VINNY WAS GOING TO COME to my side of the park and try to recruit my toms and mollies to what amounted to the feline mafia on the other side of the park, then I was going to sit back and enjoy the show. Little did he know how loyal my minions were to me. Well, except maybe Sass. And if she wanted to find out if the mice were tastier on the other side, she was welcome to. I'd been waiting for that obnoxious diva to get out of my fur for a while now.

My tail twitched as Vinny sweet-talked Sass in the shadow of the looming tree. Hours ago, when the park was still open and we were still on the downlow, the tree was all lit up. But now it was a dark, towering giant reaching up toward the glowing full moon. Its long, articulated limbs cast shadows all around the central courtyard area—our home turf.

The bipeds were doing their nightly cleaning routine, and we were hunting mice. That was our job and what we were good at.

I didn't have to hunt mice anymore, though I did sometimes just for kicks. I operated in more of a supervisory capacity these days. I'd paid my dues, and now I had my underlings to carry on the family business. *Work smarter, not harder*, my daddy always said.

My brother, Moony, helped me keep tabs on all the tabbies, calicos, and solid-colored cats under my proverbial thumb. *"Proverbial" because we don't have thumbs—get it?*

We had the mollies: Amber, Ziti, Daisy and the aforementioned Sass. And we had the toms: Moony, Hank, Cool, and Ice.

Vinny crossed over into our territory on occasion, but he was affiliated with the clowder on the south side of the park, near the entrance and parking lots. The leader over there was Scar, so named, not only for the *Lion King* villain, but also the jagged scar that ran down the side of his face and right through his left eye. Legend had it he'd rumbled with an alligator back in the day, and it cost him vision in that eye. What was left was an unseeing milky-white orb.

Scar was, in a word, a scumbag. You didn't want to mess

with him because he wasn't nice, he wasn't reasonable, and every decision he made was completely self-serving. He didn't care about the well-being of the other cats in his clowder. All he cared about was making sure he got the most food, the most power, and the most notoriety of all the cats in Fairytale Forest—and there were about two hundred of us.

The numbers fluctuated because cats came and went. Sometimes cats messed up and were lured in by the bipeds, cozying up to them for treats or scritches behind the ear—you know, those hard-to-reach areas. My own mom was carried off by one of the cat wranglers a few years ago when she let one of the janitors pick her up and use her gloriously long nails in that sensitive spot right behind the ears and down the neck. Mama was purring so loud, I heard her from behind the bushes where our clowder hung out during the day when the park was thick with bipeds.

That was the last I saw of her.

My cats knew better than to get too close to the bipeds. Our job was to rid the park of vermin, and we had the smarts and the skills to do just that.

I heard a hiss and a screech in the alley further down Storybook Street, and my instincts kicked in. I wasn't a fan of running, but before I knew it, my paws were pounding the pavement to track down the source of the noise. I needed to make sure none of my cats were in trouble again. A few of these dolts—well, as I said, I had to keep tabs on them.

I found Moony backing a rather aggressive-looking rat up against a metal dumpster the Magical Mushroom restaurant emptied its leftovers into.

"You need help, Bro?" I called out.

His whiskers twitched as he dipped his chin in acknowledgment. His green eyes shifted quickly to the side and back, sending me instructions. With a high-pitched trill, I dispatched a help signal to summon the troops.

The rat reeked—clearly afraid for its life as its fur stood on end and its tail froze in place. Its nostrils flared as it tried to figure a way out, but soon it was surrounded as Amber, Ziti, and Ice arrived, licking their lips and taking their places in an arc just inches away from our trapped prey.

"It's not going to end well for this guy," Moony joked as he looked over his shoulder at me with a smug, self-satisfied smirk.

"On three," I announced.

I counted down from three, and then it was all over for Mr. Rat.

Two

Wwhen I made my way to the custodial services building for the staff meeting, I heard shouting coming from an office down the hall. I paused to listen before heading into the staff lounge where the meeting was taking place.

It sounded like Heather's voice. I couldn't help it. Given the rumors, I was interested in hearing what she had to say. I moved a little closer. The door was cracked open an inch or two, but I couldn't see who was inside.

"I don't care what you think. I do what I want," her deep Southern drawl drifted out the crack in the door. "You should know that by now. It's a mistake to try to control me because *I'm* the one in control."

A short silence followed. If someone in the office was responding to her, I couldn't hear their voice.

"You're gonna regret messing with me," she said. "Mark my words…"

"WELL, THAT WAS TWENTY MINUTES OF MY LIFE I'M NEVER getting back," Gloria complained as she stood up and straightened the scarf on her head.

I was fighting off a yawn. "Leave it to Heather to make an issue out of toilet paper."

"I know that's right," Gloria agreed with a *tsk-tsk* sound. "The whole thing smells like bullcrap to me."

Jayden wandered over. "So we can leave now, can't we? It's six-twenty."

"Yes, dear. We can clock out." I led the procession to the time clock.

Fairytale Forest was not exactly the most technologically advanced workplace—see my earlier statement on "if it ain't broke, don't fix it." See also: "waste not, want not." The time clock was the old-fashioned punch card variety that had been used since the park opened.

That glorious sound of the ink printing on the card was music to my ears. We headed toward the back of the building, but we didn't get very far.

Heather and Walter were blocking our path.

I sighed. All I wanted to do at this point was go to bed. A woman my age needed her beauty sleep. "Is something wrong?"

Walter had an imposingly tall figure and arms like an orangutan, they were so long. He was balding on the sides so badly, the hair in the middle nearly looked like a mohawk sticking up off his head. And it was orangey-red in color, which only furthered the whole orangutan analogy. Those monkey arms crossed over his puffed-out chest. As soon as he opened his mouth, though, any intimidation would go poof into thin air.

Heather stood next to him with a scowl on her overly made-up face. She was singlehandedly keeping the eyeliner and mascara companies in business with her thick-rimmed eyes and falsie lashes. Her reddish-blonde hair was teased like it was 1988, or she was trying to appear taller than her five-foot-three stature.

"Well?" I stopped and cocked my hip out, my foot tapping impatiently. "We're way past time to go home, and we've clocked out. The Forests have a no overtime policy, remember?"

Walter finally spoke. He looked as though he'd have a deep, booming voice, but it was actually high-pitched and whining, the kind that cracked on occasion like a teenage boy's. "Heather has brought it to my attention that you two were snickering during her meeting."

The dayshift supervisor's nostrils flared as she stared us up and down, trying to look intimidating. She was in her forties. Her figure was top-heavy with bird legs, the silhouette only exaggerated by her voluminous hair. She nodded when Walter made his statement.

It required every ounce of strength I could muster to keep my eyes from rolling. Gloria looked as though she was similarly strained. Jayden's dark brows were arched with worry, his eyes darting back and forth between Walter and Heather.

"Well, I'm sorry if I can't take a meeting about toilet paper seriously," I finally responded, trying—unsuccessfully—to keep the snark out of my tone.

"Well, you should," Heather snapped. "We have to cut

down on toilet paper consumption in the park. Mr. Forest says the costs of paper products have skyrocketed this year, and we cannot afford to increase the budget."

"Maybe you should take that up with Dining Services?" Gloria quipped, looking rather proud of herself.

Walter sighed. "Ladies, I understand the entertainment factor, but please, just watch how you stock the restrooms. We should never have more than one roll in each stall. If there's not as much available, guests won't use as much. It just means monitoring the restrooms more often."

"Sounds like that mostly falls on day shift then," I pointed out. "We're not the ones here while guests are using too much TP."

"Be that as it may," Heather said in her high-and-mighty tone, "I had a talk with Karen about how night shift custodial tends to overstock the restrooms with paper towels and toilet paper. Do better in the future."

"Duly noted," I said, then coughed over another comment that was wildly inappropriate but undoubtedly hilarious.

Gloria giggled and elbowed me in the ribs. We were acting more like twelve-year-olds than women in their fifties and sixties, respectively.

"Do you see what I mean?" Heather sneered at Walter. "Complete and total lack of respect for authority."

Walter ignored her and stepped to the side to let us pass. "Have a nice day, ladies. We'll see you tonight."

I muttered something else inappropriate as we side-stepped them both and headed for our cars. Jayden followed along like a puppy dog. He was a good kid. I wondered if he'd tell his parents about this little interaction.

I didn't care. What were they going to do? Fire me after twenty years of faithful service cleaning their park?

I'd like to see them try.

I just wanted to go home and take a load off. Catch some Z's. Then I'd be back to do it all over again.

ZOE

I AWOKE FROM AN ABSOLUTELY STELLAR NAP. A cat nap, if you will. Since I am a cat, and we spend a good twelve to sixteen hours a day snoozing, it was fitting. And so would you if you could—don't even try to deny it.

The small bipeds and their progenitors appeared to be thinning out. That meant it was nearly time for myself and my fellow felines to go on the prowl for vermin. My stomach was rumbling as I slinked over to the bush my brother was curled up beneath.

"Hey, Moony, you getting up or what?"

His eyes opened, and he blinked a few times before rising to his paws. He stretched his legs out, then arched his back before sitting on his haunches and staring at me, his whiskers twitching. "Something smells weird."

"That's just Hank." I tilted my head toward the thick lump of ginger fur a few feet away. He was the heaviest cat in our clowder. He wasn't too good at chasing prey, but if he happened to sit on one—well, then he was in business.

"He must have eaten something rotten." Moony's tail

waved back and forth like a flag of surrender as he exited the bushes and stepped onto the path.

We were on the edge of our territory, over near the Gingerbread Man ride. The old wooden roller coaster was still in full swing, making a clickety-clacking racket as it whipped by us. I hoped none of the bipeds spotted us, but we tended to blend in with the thick foliage.

Amber, Cool, and Ice came from the other side, near the Goblin Go-Karts. Cool was limping. Oh no.

"Hey, Mr. Cool Cat, you okay?" I looked our seniormost member up and down as he approached, flanked by the two younger cats. Amber was a light yellow-striped tabby with amber eyes, and Ice was a blue-point Siamese who had definitely been someone's pet—not feral like most of us. But he didn't talk about his past.

Cool sat up tall and licked his lips. "Never been better," he insisted. He had to be fifteen, sixteen years old, and he had been here his whole life. He was a formidable gray-striped tabby when I first met him, but his fur was thinning, and his skeleton was starting to show. He still thought he was a young tom, though, and tried to keep up with Moony and Ice. To be fair, he could definitely beat Hank in a race, but that wasn't saying much.

"We all ready for the night?" I surveyed my crew. "Where's Ziti and Daisy? And Sass." I was secretly hoping Sass had crossed enemy lines and joined Scar and Vinny's clowder.

"No clue," Moony answered. "It's not my job to keep track of them."

It was going to be a night of perpetual eye rolling. I could just sense it. "Well, I hope they're not getting into trouble."

Before we could meow another word, fireworks began exploding overhead. It was closing time, and this was the park's farewell sequence—loud music and colorful sparkling blooms in the sky. It hurt my ears, but at least it meant we would soon have the run of the park. We all hunkered down while the show played. All the guests gathered in the courtyard around the tree, which was close to our napping spot.

I was a little miffed that my other mollies hadn't reported for duty. I had no doubt Sass was responsible for their absence. Ziti and Daisy were both younger and followers, though Ziti would certainly come into her own as she grew and gained more self-confidence. She was small-boned with delicate features and a tabby coat with a white vest and paws. Daisy was a long-haired calico and dumber than a box of rocks. I worried about that girl. She was afraid of mice and never hunted alone.

As the fireworks ended and the stampede of bipeds rushed for the exits, a trill sounded toward the tree. My ears pricked, and my hackles rose as my crew surrounded me. We'd have to go check it out.

"It better not be Vinny again," Moony said as he fell in step behind me. We presented a united front, me in the middle, Cool and Moony on either side of me, and just on our tails, Ice, Amber and Hank—who'd finally roused his stinky butt out of his napping spot.

We made it to the tree, which was still lit up. Silhouetted against the shifting pink, purple, blue and green lights was a large cat—I thought a tom at first by the size, but then I got a sharp whiff of female. She slinked from the shadows with Sass, Ziti, and Daisy following right behind her.

"Who do we have here?" she said to me.

To me?!

Who at Fairytale Forest didn't know who I was?

"I'm Zoe. I'm in charge of this sector. And who might you be?" I made myself as tall as possible, my tail twitching as I took in the chocolate-colored Persian who had taken to grooming herself as though I wasn't worth the crud under her claws.

Her amber-colored eyes narrowed. "I'm Princess."

"Isn't she pretty?" Daisy sighed in apparent awe, clearly enamored with the newcomer's silky mane.

"She just got here today," Sass filled us in. "She should get the night off to settle in."

I took a moment to consider her statement as I took care of an itch on my left paw. *No*—that was my immediate thought. I didn't care how "pretty" Miss Princess was, we all hunted. That was why we were here.

"She's been resting long enough. The park just closed, and I've already caught a scent over in the Haunted Wood. We're headed that way now. We will all be hunting together."

Before Sass or Priss—I mean Princess—could argue, all of our ears simultaneously rotated toward a blood-curdling scream.

"That came from the front of the park," Moony said as soon as silence fell again.

"New plan," I decided. "We're gonna go check it out. Let's go."

Another scream carried on the humid night air as we raced toward its source. A biped was in trouble…

Three

"I hope you have the toilet paper situation under control," Gloria joked as she joined me outside the women's restroom across from the Charms and Curses Courtyard.

"Oh, I have successfully battled the TP monster," I assured her, which sparked a cackle from my friend as we wheeled our carts across the courtyard toward the tree. Tonight we had to go up in the tree and clean the air tram transfer station. Day shift left a note that a drink was spilled up there, and the floors were sticky.

We always got the fun assignments, you know?

"At least it's a drink and not puke," Gloria pointed out. She was good at finding the silver linings in all the clouds that hung over the park.

It wasn't so bad, not really. People were just messy. And they were on vacation. They didn't want to take the time to clean up after themselves. Not to mention the fact that accidents happened, and they happened more often when there were more kids around. And most of the visitors to Fairytale Forest were of the child variety.

We took the escalator to the level of the tree housing the station for the air tram that traveled to other areas of the park. The individual cars were decorated to look like winged creatures: eagles, crows, bats, dragons, and pegasus. The cables they traveled on looked like enormous vines sprouting off the giant tree in the center of the park.

"This escalator *mumble mumble*!" Gloria put her hands over her ears. "We *mumble mumble* Hank to *mumble mumble*."

"I can't hear you!" I shook my head, brows furrowed as I attempted to piece together the few words I'd understood with the ones I didn't. The escalator was so loud! We needed to ask Hank to come look at it.

When we reached the platform, she repeated herself.

"That's what I just said!" I giggled. "Well, in my head."

"Do you want to start on that side, and I'll start on this one?" She pointed across the platform. "We don't know where the spill is, so I figured we'd mop the whole thing."

"Sounds good." I walked over to my side and looked out the windows over the whole park. Some of the buildings still had their lights on, but others were turned off already. The front of the park looked dark, even though the lights usually stayed on there all night long.

"Hey, the cats are out early tonight." I pointed toward the bushes where a cluster of furry beasts appeared to be marching toward the front of the park.

Gloria shook her head from the other side of the platform. "Those cats are always up to something."

"Hey, they do their jobs." I smiled. I thought it was neat

that the Forests used cats as natural exterminators in their park. What a brilliant idea. The feline staff kept to themselves during the day, sleeping and staying out of the guests' sight. At night, they came to life and prowled the premises, keeping the mice and rats at bay. And snakes. I'd seen dead snakes being devoured by a horde of kitties a couple of times in my tenure at Fairytale Forest. The memory gave me a shudder.

We finished the mopping and did some general cleaning, as well as emptying the trash cans all through the tree. I was tired by the time we were done, and our shift was half over already.

"Should we take our break now?" Gloria suggested as if she could read my mind.

"I like the way you think, lady." I peeled off my gloves and tossed them in the bin before steering my cart to the janitor closet in the staff-only area. Gloria followed, then we hopped aboard the noisy escalator and started our descent to the next level. We changed escalators and continued making our way down.

"Did you see the lights were off in the front of the park?" I asked as we stepped out into the damp night. It had sprinkled while we were in the tree, and the colorful lights that remained on reflected on the wet pavement of Storybook Street. Despite some low, hazy clouds, the full moon was rising in the sky, a giant pearl casting a silver spell over the entire park.

"I did notice that." Gloria shook her head. "That's definitely unusual."

When we reached the courtyard, the gaggle of cats I'd seen in almost military formation heading toward the front of the park was now approaching the tree. Zoe was the leader. The beautiful long-haired cat with silvery-gray fur and expressive green eyes was one of my favorites in the park. The cats tended to shy away from humans, even their handlers, but we'd made eye contact a few times, and she didn't shirk away from me like some of the others did.

Gloria and I walked over to where we'd stored our other carts so we didn't have to take them up in the tree. I was surprised to see Zoe had left her fellow felines and was sauntering toward me.

I expected her to head off into the bushes, but she didn't. She walked straight up to me and brushed up against my leg, rubbing the length of her body across my shin, then turning and coming back to do the other side. Meanwhile, her entourage sat and watched from a distance. A few were licking themselves, and the others were looking on intently, as though they were watching a performance.

"She's awfully friendly tonight!" Gloria exclaimed. "I thought they weren't supposed to have contact with any humans in the park except their handlers."

"They're not." I thought she'd scamper away if I bent down to pet her, but she didn't. She continued to nuzzle against me as I stroked her thick, silky fur. "She's so soft. What a pretty girl!" I hadn't had a pet in a long time. Maybe it was time I got my own cat. I'd love to have one who looked like Zoe.

"Okay, pretty girl," I told her, "Gloria and I need to get back to work. Hope you and your comrades have a successful hunt tonight." I straightened back up to my full height and wrapped my hands around the handle of my cart. We needed to empty the trash bins in the Dragon's Lair Restaurant and mop down the floor.

But Zoe followed me, getting between my legs so I was

forced to stop walking. "Sheesh! She's acting awfully strange tonight!"

"She apparently needs some affection," Gloria pointed out as she stopped her cart alongside mine.

Zoe sat right in front of my cart and looked up at me, her green eyes glowing in the dark. Then a very odd thing happened.

A voice said, "Hey, you need to follow me. Need to show you something."

I turned toward Gloria. "What? I didn't hear you again."

Her brows furrowed, making her entire forehead wrinkle up. "Woman, I didn't say a dang thing."

"Are you sure? Someone just said I needed to follow them—it was a woman's voice." I looked around but didn't see anyone except Jayden coming out of the men's restroom on the corner.

Zoe remained planted in front of the cart, her tail twitching as she stared at me intently.

Then I heard the voice again—this time it sounded like it was coming from inside my head. "Follow me! Need to show you something."

"Did you hear it that time?" I asked Gloria. "Asking me to follow?"

"Are you on something, Cat? No one is talking!" She shook her head. "Do I need to fetch the Root Doctor for you, girl?"

I stared at her, blinking. "The what doctor?"

She waved her hand at me. "It's a Gullah thing." Her lips pursed. "You're scaring me, Cat."

"It's me. Zoe," said the voice. "Trying to get you to follow me. Please? Don't know what else to do."

Okay. Perhaps Gloria was right. Perhaps I did need a doctor. I was hearing the cat talk?

So far, I'd had all the usual symptoms of menopause: hot flashes, memory lapses, joint pain, insomnia. Was hearing voices one I'd missed on the pamphlet from my doctor?

Surely I wasn't actually hearing one of the Fairytale Forest cats TALK to me!

ZOE

Sheesh! I didn't know these bipeds would be so dense. My next step was to jump up on the female and literally ride her like a horse to the disturbing sight we just saw near the front of the park. We heard the scream and rushed over there like furry missiles hurtling through the thick lowcountry night air.

The biped female—whose name was ironically "Cat"—bent down and got right in my face, making my whiskers twitch. "You want me to follow you?"

"Duh, that's what I've been trying to tell ya, lady." My tail waved in the air as I marched forward. "You guys coming?" I glanced over at my clowder. They fell into formation behind me as we paraded down the main street.

The sound of the carts' wheels rumbling behind us confirmed Cat and her coworker Gloria were on our tails. I'd been watching Cat work the entire time I'd been at Fairytale Forest, and I knew she would be able to handle what we were about to show her. She would know what to do, who to call, and how to get everything cleaned up all spick-and-span.

And we were going to hang out nearby while she did it because I had a feeling the scene would attract any opportunistic vermin who might be in the vicinity.

We arrived, and I took the lead, directing my mollies and toms to sit behind me with just a flick of my ear. Cat's shriek pierced the night air as her eyes fell upon the prone figure with a mess of blonde curls obscuring her face.

"Oh no!" she gasped, and her companion seemed equally shocked.

At least we'd done what we could do. Cat would take care of it from here.

Four

CATHERINE

Something didn't feel right fifty yards out, and as we drew closer and my brain clicked on, I realized the figure on the pavement was a person. My heart began to pound. Did the cats really lead me to a body? Was I dreaming?

"Oh no," I gasped.

Gloria halted midstride, her cart squeaking to an abrupt stop. "Is that what I think it is?"

"I think it's a body," I whispered.

My eyes darted all around this part of the park to see if anyone was nearby. I thought a flash of red streaked by around fifty yards ahead, but I wasn't sure. I already feared my ears were playing tricks on me when I heard the cat speak. Were my eyes playing tricks on me too?

As we grew closer, reddish-blonde hair and a pair of gray trousers and a white dress shirt came into view. "I think it's Heather!"

Gloria nodded, her hands clasped over her mouth like she wasn't able to speak. She was visibly trembling as she leaned against the cart, clearly not taking this discovery well. The cats were all lined up by the manicured hedge that lined the front of The Bullseye Arcade.

I guess it's up to me to figure out what to do.

I stared up at the night sky, reverently taking in the sight of the full moon shining down on us, and sent up a silent prayer for guidance. Taking a deep breath, I slipped on a fresh pair of gloves. Then I slowly approached the body and crouched down, my knees creaking and protesting as my weight shifted forward. Using my gloved hand, I pulled the blonde curls away from the figure's face to check if the eyes were open or closed.

Eerie, lifeless green eyes with gold flecks stared back at me.

Trying not to panic, I grabbed her wrist and felt for a pulse. I shook my head, not feeling anything. Her skin was already cold and turning a dull color.

"Is she…dead?" a voice came from behind us.

I whipped around to find Jayden standing there. Adrenaline surging through me, I leaped to my feet. "You scared the crap out of me, Jay!"

"Is she…" he repeated, but he left out the D word.

I slowly nodded. "I think so. Can you call 9-1-1 and then your dad?"

"Okay." He fumbled for his phone, and I did the same.

"Walter?" I said as calmly as I could when he answered the phone. It probably didn't sound as calm as I hoped, but I tried.

"What's wrong? Where's Karen?" he grumbled. I'd clearly woken him from a dead sleep.

Ugh. Probably best not to use that word right now.

"Oh…Karen…right…"

Karen *was* my immediate supervisor. The night-shift custodial supervisor. *Oopsie.* Probably should have contacted her on my walkie-talkie before calling Walter. I just wasn't used to her actually being helpful in ordinary circumstances—so it was hard to imagine she would be helpful in what appeared to be extraordinary circumstances.

Gloria to the rescue. She held up her walkie and mouthed, "I'll call her."

"What's wrong?" Walter repeated. "Did something happen?" He was becoming a little more lucid now.

"Um, Walter, I don't know how to tell you this, but—"

"Just spit it out, Catherine." He used my full name. That meant he was beyond irritated.

I gulped in a deep breath before spitting it out: "Heather has suffered an unfortunate accident."

"What do you mean 'unfortunate'? Why is she even there? She should have left hours ago!" He sounded panicked.

After that, I heard a garble of voices. He must have put his hand over the phone. He was probably talking to his wife. Then his voice came back, louder and stronger. "Is she okay?"

My stomach flip-flopped as I stared down at her body on the pavement. Sirens began to scream in the distance—Jayden's 9-1-1 call had worked.

"No, Walter, she's not okay. She's dead."

IT WAS ORGANIZED PANDEMONIUM—*IF THAT'S A THING*—AS the medics arrived, then the police, then the coroner, and, finally, a detective. Then another detective.

After the body was removed and the area was cordoned off with yellow police tape, Gloria and I were summoned to the executive offices above Guest Services near the entrance to the park.

As we headed that way, Gloria stopped by the restroom while I waited outside. I noticed Zoe the cat saunter out from between two buildings and walk right up to me. I'd never noticed she was interested in humans before tonight. But she'd…communicated…with me earlier, right? I couldn't have been imagining that.

She sat and stared at me, her green eyes steady and watchful. "Thank you for listening to me. Sorry about your…friend," I heard in my head.

Her mouth didn't move. Her whiskers didn't even twitch, but I heard a smooth, middle-aged-sounding woman's voice in my head. And it wasn't my own. It was deeper, and it didn't have that Charleston drawl I got from my daddy that I'd never quite been able to rid myself of.

"Are you really talking to me?" I asked her.

"Are *you* really talking to *me*?" she returned.

"We're both crazy, aren't we?" I joked with her.

"Speak for yourself, biped." She bent down and licked her paw. "I've always been able to understand bipeds. They just don't usually take the time to listen to me."

Gloria came out of the restroom and tossed a wad of

paper towels in the trash. "Didn't want to fill the trash up in there." She acknowledged the cat with a smile. "She's a pretty one, isn't she?"

I hadn't admitted to my work bestie that I'd been conversing with a cat, and now wasn't the right time. We needed to get to the conference room before Walter had a heart attack. He sounded upset on the walkie when he summoned us.

I couldn't blame him. Heather had been working here for a while. Gloria shared the rumor going around that they were involved, but Walter was married. His wife, Carol, was the sweetest thing—she always baked cookies and doled out gift cards during the holidays. The gift cards were for the clothing boutique she owned on King Street in the Charleston historic district, where even a pair of earrings cost $50, but, you know, "it's the thought that counts."

A few cops were milling about on Storybook Street, and there were two more inside the Guest Services building. We headed up to the conference room on the third floor where we'd been instructed to meet Walter and the detective. The aroma of freshly brewed coffee filled my senses as I stopped to knock three times on the open door.

"Here they are," Walter said, rising from the conference table. "These are the ladies who discovered the body."

I had to stop myself from blurting out that, actually, Zoe the Cat had been the one to find the body—or one of her feline associates. But I managed to save myself that embarrassment.

The detectives were quite a pair. The man was short with waxy skin and a generous build. The woman was tall and lanky, the boxy dress shirt she wore concealing any evidence of curves. She was the one who greeted us. "I'm

Detective Shelly Towers," she said, "and this is my partner, Frank Powers."

"Powers and Towers?" I repeated, incredulous. Gloria snickered next to me.

"Yeah, we get that a lot." She gestured toward the chairs across from them. "Please, have a seat. We just have a few questions for you."

We settled ourselves in, and I noticed the two conferring over a yellow legal pad as though they were trying to decide who was asking the questions and who was taking notes. Shelly won. I supposed Detective Powers wasn't the one in *power* after all.

"I understand you ladies work on the janitorial team," she asked.

We both nodded. "Custodial," Gloria corrected.

"Tell us how you came to find Ms. Heather Suka's body," Shelly questioned.

Gloria deferred to me. I decided to leave out the part where Zoe practically begged us to follow her. "Uh, we just were heading toward the front of the park and discovered her body on the street."

The detective's already slitty eyes narrowed even further. "Why were you heading toward the front of the park?"

I looked at Gloria, who shrugged. "Uh, just routine stuff. Checking to make sure things were spick-and-span, you know. Doing our jobs."

"Also, the lights at the front of the park were off," Gloria added. "They aren't normally turned off. So we wondered what was going on up here."

Oh, right! Good job, Gloria. I shot her a smile.

"Did you hear anything coming from that area of the park?" the detective asked.

I shook my head. "No, ma'am. But we were up in the tree, and the escalator is very loud."

"Up in the tree?" Her eyes darted to Walter, who cleared his throat.

"The large tree that serves as the centerpiece of the park," he explained.

"So you didn't hear anything and just noticed the lights were out?" she repeated.

I nodded. "It's unusual for the lights to go off at the entrance during the night shift."

"What did you see when you first arrived? Did you touch the body?" she asked.

"I checked to see if she was still breathing," I reported, rushing through the memories I'd recorded of the moment. Just thinking about it again made my skin crawl with goose-bumps. "Oh—I saw a flash of red. I think someone was leaving the park when we arrived on scene. Someone wearing red?"

"Flash of red?" Detective Powers repeated. Then he hastily scrawled a note on the yellow legal pad.

"I saw it too," Gloria corroborated my story. "Like a red shirt or something."

"Where's Karen?" I turned to Walter, who still looked shell-shocked at the other end of the table. "She never answered her walkie-talkie."

"She went home sick around midnight," he answered, shaking his head.

"Oh, she was wearing a red shirt when she came in," I remembered.

Karen and Heather had never gotten along. They were

quibbling about something before the start of the meeting yesterday as well. But surely Karen wouldn't have hurt Heather? Heather died of natural causes…right?

"So what happened to her? Heather, I mean." I turned back to the detectives. "Heart attack?"

"We don't know yet. Her body is with the medical examiner now," Detective Powers spoke up again. Something flashed through his eyes—something accusatory as he looked at me. "Mr. McDuff reported that you had an altercation with Ms. Suka earlier in the day."

"What?!" My eyes snapped to Walter's, and he immediately looked away. "It wasn't an altercation. I just didn't appreciate that we were held after work with no overtime pay for a pointless meeting about toilet paper usage."

Gloria started to laugh but then coughed to cover it up. Walter shot her a glare, but he still wouldn't make eye contact with me.

"Did you and Heather Suka have an adversarial relationship?" Detective Towers continued the questioning.

"Adversarial?" I tapped my fingernails on the shiny wood-grain surface of the conference room table. "Um… not any more so than any other employee in this park. She isn't exactly well-liked here."

"Wasn't," Gloria corrected.

"Right. Karen and Heather didn't get along either. And there were plenty of others she rubbed the wrong way," I explained. "Why are you asking? Are you trying to say there was foul play?"

Detective Powers and Towers exchanged looks. "We aren't at liberty to divulge details at this time, but we are going to have to ask you and your colleagues not to leave town. We may have follow-up questions as our investigation unfolds."

Investigation?

Did they think Heather was murdered?

ZOE

I ASSEMBLED MY TOMS AND MOLLIES NEAR THE TREE later that night. "Give me the report."

My brother stepped forward. "I stationed myself near the fallen biped. More bipeds in uniforms came to haul her away on a cart covered by a drape. I think that means the female was deceased."

I probed further: "Did anyone talk to the cats in that territory? Did they see anything?"

"Scar and Vinny were in the area," Hank reported. "But they aren't talkin'."

"What were they doing there? That's not their area," I protested.

"Why do we care?" Priss—I refused to call her Princess—slinked out from behind Sass and Daisy, her tail curling seductively as she sashayed over to me, her chocolate mane ruffling in the breeze. "I thought we were here to catch mice."

"I'll tell you why," Mr. Cool Cat asserted himself as the senior member of the group. "If something bad happens in the park, it could get shut down..."

"So?" Priss blinked repeatedly, her right ear flicking a couple times as though she was perturbed.

"No bipeds, no food, no rodents," Cool summed it up for her.

Priss had been silenced. I wasn't upset about this development. I'd just met her, and she was already driving me crazy. She sashayed over to Moony and rubbed up against him. Ziti shot her a dirty look.

Was Priss flirting with my brother?

Moony ignored her and focused his attention on me. "What should we do now?" *That'a boy.*

"Wherever you go," Priss purred in Moony's general direction, "I'm going too."

I rolled my eyes. "Ice and Moony, you—and only you—go back to the front of the park and see what's happening. We only have a few hours before dawn. The night shift should be clocking out, and day shift should be clocking in soon. I want to know what happens when the bipeds switch shifts."

"Aye, aye, Captain." My brother dipped his chin, and he and Ice took off toward the front of the park.

"What about the rest of us?" Amber looked restless as her tail twitched back and forth. She always wanted in on the action.

Hank had assumed his usual loaf-of-bread position. "I'm gonna take a nap. I caught a mouse earlier, so I'm good for the night."

Ziti scoffed. "I think you mean *I* caught a mouse and shared it with you." She was one of the best mousers in our clowder, so I had no doubt she spoke the truth.

"I'm going to go see if I can talk to Vinny," I decided. "See what he knows. I just have a bad feeling about this…"

"Why?" Sass questioned. "We've seen bipeds get carried out of here before. You know, after they get hurt in the park."

"This is different. Moony said they covered her body. She may have died," I reminded her.

"Maybe she just got sick?" Amber asserted.

I remembered the panic on the faces of the two bipeds I'd alerted. "Or maybe she just got murdered…"

Five

CATHERINE

Sleeping was not in the cards for me. My phone rang at nine o'clock, and it was Detective Towers, asking me to come into the station for additional questioning. I thought about calling Gloria to see if she got the same summons, but A) I didn't want to wake her up if she hadn't, and B) I didn't want to worry her. Gloria was the Mother Hen of the custodial department, and she worried about all of us—even Heather, for some odd reason.

I, on the other hand, was the rebellious teenage daughter of the group, complete with the attitude problem and smart mouth. Even though I was too old to be Gloria's daughter, she did try to "mother" me at times. Like when she worried I didn't have enough social interaction in my life outside of work.

"Do your kids come to visit?" she asked me one time.

"Nope. One lives in California, and the other is in New York. No, I don't go to visit them either."

Her frown was enough to make me sad—and it was my own sob story!

"Grandkids?" she probed. "FaceTime?"

"Nope, no grandkids. Not yet anyway."

My two sons were focused on their careers, and any romantic entanglements they'd had were quickly dissolved due to their impatience with flighty and indecisive women. "You just haven't met the right one yet," I always assured them. It *had* to be the women, right? My sons were definitely "catches."

One was a computer programmer, and the other did something with maps that was way over my head. Actually, both of their jobs were over my head. They got their analytical brains from their father, or so I always believed. I'd been told my whole life that I wasn't very bright. Oh, and it was pounded into my brain from an early age that girls are bad at math.

I stayed home with my sons when they were young, so I never went to college. I'd thought about taking some classes. History and social sciences like sociology and psychology had always appealed to me. Anthropology was intriguing to me too.

But here I was at fifty-five, still working the same job I'd gotten back when my boys went off to school all those years ago. They were probably too embarrassed to tell their friends their mom was a janitor.

A couple years back when Karen was hired, I thought I might get her job. But they moved her into the position from the food services division. She wasn't a fan favorite, though she was slightly more tolerable than Heather. I was always thanking my lucky stars that I worked for Karen and not Heather.

I got dressed and climbed into my gray Nissan Rogue, heading for the city. Driving in downtown Charleston was not my cup of tea, but I didn't have much choice. Now, I loved *walking* around the city. It was a city that begged to be walked. The architecture was to die for, and every nook and cranny were bursting with charm and history. From the clip-clopping of horses leading tourists on carriage rides, the eye-popping pastel homes on Rainbow Row, the fragrant blooms of myrtle and magnolias, the warm breezes blowing off the Battery, to the delicious smells wafting out of award-winning eateries, it was a feast for one's senses.

However, going to the police station for questioning was not on my Fun Day in Charleston itinerary.

I found parking a block away, which wasn't bad for a Thursday morning, and headed into the modern-looking building that appeared out of place next to its neighbors. Beelining for the reception desk, I tried not to make eye contact with any of the figures bustling around the lobby area.

The bored-looking receptionist was on the phone when I approached. She held up one finger. It became immediately apparent she was on a personal call—something about her nail appointment getting canceled, and she had a broken nail. A crisis of epic proportions, obviously.

Finally, she hung up and lifted a plastic smile to me. "Can I help you, hon?"

"Hi, I have a meeting with Detective Towers." I felt like "I've been ordered to appear for questioning" sounded a little suspicious. My eyes fell on the nameplate on the desk behind her. Kid you not, it said Cpl. Winston Flowers.

"Flowers? Does everyone have rhyming names around here?" I chuckled, trying to alleviate the nervousness I was feeling. And I didn't know why. It wasn't like I had anything to hide.

"Well, bless your heart," Receptionist Lady quipped. But she didn't acknowledge my witty sense of humor. Her last name must have been SOURS.

She instead pressed another button on her phone, mumbled something into the receiver and then pointed to the right. "Down that hall, last door on the left."

I nodded and thanked her—she was just doing her job, after all. If I had to deal with people all day long, I would probably be crabby too. I actually preferred dealing with trash.

What did that say about humankind?

I was still amusing myself with my funny internal thoughts. I needed to take that energy right to Detective Towers if she was going to come at me. I didn't really have anything to report other than what I shared the night before.

"Thank you for coming in, Ms. Lyon. You can have a seat right there." She pointed to the chair across from her desk. I noticed Detective Powers was not joining us.

"What can I do for you?" I folded my hands in my lap.

Her smile was forced and stiff. "I'd like to know more about your relationship with Heather Suka. How long had you worked together?"

Just got here, and I was already wary of the direction this was headed. "Um…I don't know…five years? Maybe more?"

"Did you ever work with her as a colleague? Like with an equal level of authority?"

I shook my head. "No, never."

"What about your immediate supervisor, Karen York?"

She didn't glance up from where she was jotting down notes.

"She's only been my supervisor for a couple years. She transferred from a different division to custodial." I shifted in the chair, crossing my legs at the ankle.

"I see. Were you aware that there are cameras all over the park recording both guests and employees?" Detective Towers continued, almost like she expected it to be surprise information.

I mean, duh. We were all aware of the cameras. We were told about the cameras on Day 1. They were meant to surveil guests, but there was no doubt they were also used to deter employees from any shenanigans.

"Of course." I nodded and smiled. "Hopefully you can figure out who is responsible for Heather's death using video footage."

She sat back with a tiny smirk curling her lips. "So you know it was murder, then." She made a note on her yellow legal pad.

I couldn't prevent my eyes from rolling. "I didn't say that. You did, last night in the conference room."

"We didn't know for sure then," she corrected me.

"You insinuated it," I defended myself. "Look, Heather had a lot of enemies. It's certainly more believable that someone offed her than she died of natural causes. She was in her forties and relatively healthy, as far as I know."

"And you were one of her enemies," the detective goaded me. "Plus, we have you in proximity to the victim around the time of her death. Your only alibi is your friend, who may have been your accomplice. Smart plan to be the ones to 'stumble upon' the body—it's a great way to cover up that you're the ones who killed her."

"What?!" I scoffed. "I might not have liked Heather, but I certainly didn't kill her! I told you, we were up in the tree cleaning. I'm sure the cameras will corroborate that. And didn't the cameras catch the killer anyway? The ones on Storybook Street? Have you checked them?"

"You tell me," Detective Towers fired back. "Which camera would have captured the footage? Tell me, and we'll check it out."

I shook my head. "I don't know where all the cameras are. I just know they're everywhere."

"Which is why you turned them off," she accused.

"Are you serious right now?" I leaned forward. My blood was beginning to boil, but I was really trying to stay calm and rational—difficult on only two hours of sleep. Was she just trying to get me angry enough to slip up and say something I shouldn't?

She laced her fingers together. "Did you turn them off?"

"No!" I laughed this time—it was that absurd. "I wouldn't even have the slightest clue how to do it. And the reason I don't know where all the cameras are is because I don't pay attention to them. I don't have anything to hide."

"I understand the security office is in the tree," Detective Towers stated. "And that's where you said you were."

"I was cleaning the platform where the sky tram boards," I said. "Gloria was with me. We were there mopping the floors and emptying the trash. Then we walked toward the front of the park."

"What made you go to the front of the park? As I understand it from your boss, Mr. Walter McDuff, you were assigned to the central area of the park last night." She cocked her head and shot me an accusatory glare. "How do we know you didn't go to the tree to turn off the cameras, then go to the front so you could murder Heather Suka? You had to leave your assigned area for *some* reason, if it wasn't to commit murder."

I didn't want to have to tell her this. I didn't really want to tell anyone. Would it sound less crazy than me just saying I had a hunch there was an issue I needed to check out at the front of the park?

"Ms. Lyon?" She blinked a few times, then her gray gaze stabbed into me. "Why did you go to the front of the park? How did you get to be the one who discovered the body if you weren't the murderer?"

"You're *sure* she was murdered." I was trying to buy myself some time while I figured out how to explain what happened in a way that didn't make me look like a raving lunatic. I wanted to help my case, not hinder it.

"She was strangled to death," Detective Towers informed.

"Strangled. Oh wow…" The thought made me shudder.

Her eyes narrowed as they stabbed into me. "But you knew that, didn't you? Just like you knew where the camera access was in the security office?"

"The cats were acting weird," I blurted out. "So I followed them. They led me right to the body."

Her brows drew together, and she stared at me, lips parted like she wanted to speak but couldn't quite find the words. Finally: "Cats?"

"Yeah, the park has a cat colony that roams the park at night, keeping the pests at bay," I explained. "They're natural exterminators. They come out when we're cleaning. Hardly anyone sees them during the day. Anyway, one of them came up to me and was rubbing on me, which they don't usually do. And then she and the other cats started marching toward—"

A single brow lifted. "Marching?"

"Well, you know, they were walking together, like in formation," I tried to explain. "Like they were on a mission."

I was obviously leaving out the part where I heard Zoe speak to me in my head.

"Go on."

"Right. Well, Gloria and I followed them down Storybook Street toward the entrance, and Heather's body came into view. That's when I ran over to her and checked to see if she was breathing. We called 9-1-1 immediately after."

She glanced down at her notes on the legal pad. "But the 9-1-1 call didn't come from you."

"No, our coworker, Jayden, who happens to be the owners' son, arrived around the same time we did. He called 9-1-1 and then his parents. And I called Walter, my boss."

"When you bent down to check if Heather was breathing, did you see her neck?" Detective Towers questioned.

"No, her hair was covering her neck and most of her face." I wrung my hands. She was strangled? How terrible. I'd be lying if I hadn't thought—at least jokingly—that I'd like to strangle her.

But *of course* I would never act on that thought! Not in a million, trillion years. Did the detective believe me?

She seemed less convinced of my guilt than a few moments ago. Was she just playing Bad Cop with me? *If that's the case, I'd like to speak with Good Cop now*, I thought.

"We're still in the process of reviewing the video footage from the cameras in the park that were functioning, as well as those in the parking lot." She jotted a few more things down on the legal pad. I couldn't read what she wrote though—her handwriting wasn't exactly neat.

"Did you talk to Karen York yet?" I asked. "She is my shift supervisor."

"She has not responded to the messages we left," Detective Towers answered. "We were told she went home sick yesterday evening shortly after clocking in."

"Well…to be honest, I'd start there." I straightened in my chair. "There was a lot of bad blood between them."

"What kind of bad blood?"

I took a deep breath, not sure how much of the ongoing drama I wanted to disclose. She was the detective—wasn't it her job to gather this intel? I was making her job too easy.

But I also wanted to know who murdered Heather. Perhaps I didn't have as many enemies as she did, but my mouth got me into trouble from time to time. Case in point: me sitting in this interrogation right now was basically because I'd gotten into it with Heather after the TP meeting. What if Heather's murderer was someone who hated me too?

And it *had* to be someone in the park, right? Because the gates were always locked after all the guests were herded out at the end of the day. Unless a guest happened to hide and stick around—but then how would they have gotten out?

"So…Heather and Karen have never liked each other," I explained. "Their feud goes back to when Karen was a manager in the food services area and was always griping about Heather's custodians not adequately cleaning the dining areas. Then Karen was moved to the custodial department, and, well, you can imagine Heather wasn't a big fan of that. Not to mention, Karen is a very stuffy, conservative, religious type, whereas Heather was, um…promiscuous? I am not sure the best word to use. She has had a lot of…um…relationships…"

"Heather wasn't married." Detective Towers glanced down at her legal pad.

"Well, no…not as of yesterday. But she'd been married and divorced three times, so we all assumed it was only a matter of time before she was walking down the aisle again."

"I see…" The detective looked down at her notes as though she was trying to figure out something else to ask so she could keep me longer.

"Can I go now? I'm supposed to be asleep right now, you know. I work the night shift," I reminded her.

"I haven't had sleep either." She immediately backed up her statement with a yawn, then covered her mouth and closed her eyes for a moment. "Sorry about that."

It immediately made me yawn too. "Yawns are contagious, you know."

"I may have follow-up questions," she warned. "But you can go for now."

I rose, feeling empathetic that she was overworked and overtired. I felt like that from time to time too, so it was relatable. She was going to uncover all sorts of interesting things once she delved into the interpersonal relationships between park employees, but at least I was out of the hot seat.

At least I hoped I was.

"Oh, Ms. Lyon," she looked up from her notes, "as a reminder: don't leave the area. We will be following up with security and reviewing the video evidence to make sure your alibi checks out."

A shiver raced up my spine. The way she said it confirmed I was indeed still in the hot seat.

Six

ZOE

"Would you quit staring at Miss Priss and pay attention to what you're doing?" I chastised my brother when I noticed his gaze wandering over to where our new member was sitting, one leg hiked in the air as she licked her unmentionable areas, her pink tongue sliding over her long, silky fur.

"Oh, sorry, Sis. Her name is Princess, by the way, not Priss."

"She's Priss as far as I'm concerned." Just what I needed was another drama queen around here, like I didn't already have Sass to deal with, not to mention Daisy the Ditz, who was following both of the divas around like a puppy dog.

"I thought you wanted to know what I found out about the biped last night." His whiskers were ruffled by a gust of wind as he stared at me out of green eyes that matched my own. I stationed him near the front of the park where the bipeds in charge of the other bipeds worked and asked him to find out what happened. It was now early morning, and he was coming to make his report.

He stood up straight and tall, his bushy gray and white tail swishing behind him. "The uniformed bipeds were swarming the place all night. Making flashes—"

"Those are cameras," I informed him.

Moony wasn't nearly as cultured or worldly as I was. I spent my formative years hanging out near the security office, where they watched screens all night long. It was boring there at night with no visitors in the park, so they switched some of the screens to things they called "TV" or "movies." There was a wealth of information about biped culture on those screens. I was fascinated by the dynamics of the male and female bipeds, not to mention the little ones, who reminded me of the tiny bipeds who were always running wild through the park and making messes with dripping ice cream cones and spilled popcorn.

"What do the flashes—I mean cameras—do?" he questioned.

The security bipeds liked to watch a lot of crime shows. *CSI*, *Law and Order*, *Criminal Minds*, for starters. I could basically work as a detective with that kind of training— and I planned to.

I needed to make sure the park wasn't shuttered. Who knew where we would all end up if it did? We'd be separated for sure. And though I wouldn't mind ditching Priss and Sass—and Vinny, Scar and the rest of the mafia cats—I didn't want to get separated from Moony or Mr. Cool Cat, or my other pals like Amber, Ziti, Hank and Ice.

"They use the cameras to take photos of the crime scene," I explained. "Did they block it off with yellow caution tape?"

He nodded. "Yeah, what is that for?"

"Just to keep other bipeds out of the crime scene."

"How do you know it was a crime?"

"Did you see the female's neck?" I shuddered, remembering how it looked.

"I guess I didn't notice. Bipeds all look the same to me." He shrugged.

Images of it flashed through my mind. "It was raw and red, looked like something had cut into it. I am pretty sure that is what killed her."

"So, another biped put something around her neck and cut off her air?" he ventured.

"That's right. You're a quick learner, Moony."

His lips spread into a grin. "Thanks, Sis." His tail swished proudly. "So now what happens?"

"Well, tell me what else you heard…"

"They're shutting down the park today," he reported.

A chill raced up my spine. "Oh no…well, that's not good."

"What difference does it make to us? It just means we don't have to hide out all day."

"Right, but if the park doesn't have visitors, then there won't be any food. Which means there won't be any food for us either. And if the owners don't make money on the park, the park won't survive. And if the press finds out—"

"Press?" His green eyes widened.

"The media, you know, like newspapers and TV stations…"

He shook his head. "I don't know what any of that is."

Little brothers. They could be so…ignorant sometimes. You know what they say: ignorance is bliss. For some cats, that was true. But I liked to be informed. I liked to know what was going on. I wanted to be in control of my own destiny.

I had a bad feeling about this incident, and I wanted to make sure it didn't affect my clowder, you know? If I didn't look out for them, who would?

"Well, what else did you find out?" I prodded.

"I don't know if this is useful, but they kept talking about someone named Karen. I'm assuming that's another biped who works here?"

I scratched my claws against the bark of a nearby tree, sharpening them. "Karen is the nightshift manager."

"Oh. Well, they were saying she went home sick yesterday," he said.

I nodded. This matched other intel I'd received. "Right."

"Though she supposedly clocked out at eight o'clock, someone said they had her on the security camera leaving at midnight." He looked especially proud of himself after this revelation.

"Midnight? That's after the murder…"

"Why would she lie?" my brother posed the obvious question.

"Guilty people lie. Good work, Moony. I'm going to head over that way this morning and see what I can find out since there won't be guests in the park." I'd tried to talk to Vinny the night before, but I didn't get anywhere with him. Hopefully I could discover some clues on my own.

"Oh, can I come too?" My brother gave me an extra-pitiful hopeful look.

I shook my head. "No, you stay here and make sure everyone gets a good sleep in so we're ready to go on the prowl tonight. You can be in charge."

My brother's eyes lit up. "In charge?" His chest puffed up. "I can handle that."

"I know you can." I briefly nuzzled his thick, long-haired mane. "Now make sure everyone stays out of trouble until I get back."

"When are *you* going to sleep?" He seemed concerned.

"Don't worry about me. I'll find a place to take a cat nap…"

CATHERINE

When I woke up to the sound of my blaring alarm, groggy from my whopping four-hour nap, I had a stunning revelation. It wasn't so much a revelation as a shoved-aside memory leaping to the forefront of my mind. That happened occasionally at my age. I would walk into a room and then forget why. I would make a mental note that something was important, and two seconds later, I was distracted by something else, and the important thing vanished into thin air.

Today's important note that I was definitely not going to forget: a flash of red near the park entrance when I arrived on the scene. And I remembered when I'd seen Karen upon my arrival for my shift, she was wearing a red shirt.

Hmm…could that be Clue #1?

Then I flashed back even farther, to right before the infamous Toilet Paper Summit. Because everything went off the rails, I'd forgotten about the conversation I overheard coming from Heather's office. She was yelling at someone—who? Something about how she was in control, and the person would regret messing with her.

Was she talking to Karen? Karen would have been in the building at that time, after all, for the meeting we were about to have.

Was Karen trying to prove that Heather was not, in fact, in control?

Killing her would sure be an effective way to assert her dominance. A little over the top, maybe, but definitely effective!

While I was taking a shower, my phone rang. I wasn't able to answer, so I let it go to voicemail, which I played as soon as I stepped out, still dripping water on my fuzzy pink bathroom rug.

Walter's nasal voice came out loud and clear, "Just wanted to let you know that the park is closed today. We've managed to keep the reason for the closure out of the media thus far, which is the way the Forests prefer to keep it, if possible. You're still due in at nine-thirty, but I wanted you to know why there wouldn't be guests in the park. We're going to do some special projects since we don't need to do the day-to-day cleaning. On another note: please do not discuss the events of last night with anyone other than law enforcement. Okay, see you tonight. I'll be in to speak to everyone on night shift at some point."

I had been wondering if the park would be able to maintain normal hours after such a tragedy on its grounds. The owners had a lot of connections in the community, and their family went waaaaaay back as long-time Charlestonians, so the fact this had stayed out of the media didn't surprise me in the least. I was fairly sure the Chief of Police was Mrs. Forest's brother or cousin or something.

I headed into the park with one goal in mind: talk to Karen. I wanted to nonchalantly butter her up and try to extract some info from her, see what she knew about the Heather Situation. I had learned a few interesting tidbits in the detective's office earlier today, and I filled Gloria in on the latest as soon as we bumped into each other at the timeclock.

"Did the detective call you?" I quizzed as she applied her Chapstick. The woman was never without her cherry lip balm. If the apocalypse happened, Gloria Bress would be A-OK as long as she had that tube of hope in her grip.

"No, child, she didn't call me!" She brushed away my question with a scoff. "She knows I'm an old woman who minds my own durn business. I'm not gonna be any help to her investigation. But evidently she thought she could crack you."

I laughed. Gloria was gifted at reading people, and I tended to agree with her. "She thought you were my accomplice."

My work bestie's hooting laugh carried down the hall as we headed for Karen's office. "I'm gonna let you do all the talking," she promised. "I'm gonna just sit there and look pretty!"

"Well, you should have no problems achieving that goal!" I patted her on the back affectionately. She was wearing a vibrant animal-print tunic today, cropped black leggings, and a matching animal-print wrap for her hair.

First we stopped by the managers' lounge because word on Storybook Street was that Walter's wife had brought in some cookies, and we could find them in the lounge. We snuck in and each grabbed one before heading to our boss's office.

"So good," I mumbled, my mouth full of cookie as we ambled down the hall.

"So good," my work bestie agreed.

Karen was filing away some paperwork when we arrived. You'd think a big theme park with state-of-the-art tech in our rides and attractions would ensure our offices at least functioned as part of the twenty-first century, but nope. The Forests were old-school when it came to business practices, so that meant we did nearly everything on paper. And we had forms out the wazoo. All different colors: green, blue, ecru, SALMON. What the heck kind of color is salmon for a paper form, anyway? Salmon is a fish, am I right? And ecru? Get outta here with that crap.

"Good evening, ladies," Karen said. She was from Minnesota, so she had one of those Midwestern accents like in the movie *Fargo*. That also meant she was a little stand-offish yet very polite and could make a mean casserole.

"Feeling better?" I prompted as we both sat in the chairs across from her desk, which was filled with pictures of her adult daughters and grandsons.

"Better?" She blinked a few times, and then a dry cough erupted. "Oh, yes, much better, thank you. I guess you had some excitement here last night?"

"Did you leave before that happened?" I asked.

"Yes," she smiled and nodded, "I wasn't feeling too well, so I left around eight."

"You were here when we got in," I reminded her. "At nine-thirty."

Gloria just barely brushed her elbow against mine as if to warn me not to get carried away.

Karen gave a nervous laugh. "Oh, right. Well, I left just after that. Sorry, I had such a bad migraine that everything from last night is a little hazy." She sighed and stuffed a stack of papers in a manila file folder.

I just barely caught a flash of the form on top, a green one. Green forms were used as internal memos among the supervisors. If I wasn't mistaken, it was Heather's signature at the bottom.

I needed to get my hands on that memo. It might explain what she and Heather were fighting about—especially if the yelling I heard just prior to the TP Meeting was directed to Karen. I'd have to figure out a way to sneak back in here at some point in time tonight.

"Do you have any idea who might have wanted to hurt Heather?" I asked next.

Karen's face drained of color, making her already pale skin look washed out and dull. "Um…no…" She lifted a finger and then forced a hacking cough, turning to aim it into her upper arm. "Sorry, I'm still not one hundred percent tonight."

"Heather had a lot of enemies, didn't she?" I continued, trying to see if I could get her to admit she was one of them.

"She certainly did. It's sad, though. She has a son, you know." She mustered up a frown.

"She does?" My ears perked up. "I didn't know that."

"Yes, he's in college." She went back to organizing things on her desk, moving her stapler closer to her phone and putting some pens back in a ceramic holder.

"I'm so sorry to hear that." I had never heard Heather talk about a son. Gloria reached out and grasped my hand, then closed her eyes. That meant she was saying a prayer, so I briefly closed my eyes and did the same.

I wasn't a fan of Heather—obviously—but her son did deserve answers. Not to mention the fact that I needed to clear my name as well.

I was invested in finding her killer. I was used to slinking around at night and digging through the trash, and I had a feeling those skills would serve me well in this endeavor.

Before I could ask anything else, a knock came on the doorframe, and Walter stepped inside. "Oh, there you three are. Karen, have you gone over tonight's assignments with everyone?"

She dipped her chin apologetically. "No, sorry. Just getting settled."

"Feeling better?" His eyebrows rose, and his tone made me think he didn't believe she'd been sick either. Looked like he was also suspicious—I wondered if he knew what Heather and Karen had been feuding over. It had to be something bigger than the toilet paper budget, right?

"Yes, much. Thanks. Can you call everyone to the lounge so I can give out assignments?" She gave him a smile, and he nodded and headed out. I heard his shoes squeaking on the shiny hallway floor. Someone had given it a good waxing. Probably someone on day shift.

"We're going to head to the lounge, ladies." She stood up as though it were a signal for us to leave. But I really wanted to get my hands on that green form in the manila folder that was still on her desk. How could I do that?

"After you." I gestured toward the door. Then I extended my legs under her desk and used one foot to step on the shoelace of my other shoe, untying it.

Karen looked a little uneasy but started for the door. I nodded to Gloria, and she stood up and followed our boss. I took a few steps, then bent down. "Hey, I gotta tie my shoe. I'll catch up in a sec."

She and Gloria headed out, and like a flash of lightning, I bolted for the file folder and grabbed the green form. Just as I was about to stuff it in my pocket, I heard the door spring open. I quickly wadded the memo up and tossed it in the trashcan. *Ugh! I was nearly caught!*

"I forgot my assignment book," she explained. Then her brows furrowed when she saw me standing by her desk. "What was that? What did you just do?"

"Oh, I found some trash under your desk when I was tying my shoe," the lie quickly sprang to my lips.

Whew!

Now she waited for me to leave before she shut the door behind me. I heard the lock engage.

I'd have to figure out a way to get back in there…

Seven

ZOE

I went to check on Moony's progress later that evening. My brother, the illustrious hunter, was chasing a lizard all around the entrance to the custo-dial building when I arrived.

"Uh, hi, I can see that you're busy right now, but when you have a moment, could you come over and give me an update?" My tail swished back and forth with annoyance as I watched him practically bounce off the stucco walls.

"Hey, Sis!" he called out, but his eyes never left the small, fast lizard who was apparently enjoying taunting him. He darted left, he darted right, and finally he ran straight up the wall. Moony jumped up, smacked right into the side of the building, and then slid down like Wile E Coyote chasing the Roadrunner in one of those old cartoons.

Oh, yeah, they watched *Looney Toons* in the security office too.

He was a little out of breath when he finally padded over to me. "What's up?"

"That's what I want to know."

"Right…so…I managed to get inside the building and headed up to the floor where the Cleaning Bipeds work," he filled me in.

"Yeah?" We'd discussed that they were called custodians or janitors, but he never remembered. I got all the brains in the family; that much was clear.

"So that female with the gray hair—the one you led to the body last night?"

"Her name is Cat, ironically." Was that why I felt an affinity with her?

"Oh, wow. That's cool. I can probably remember that…"

I was pretty sure I'd already told him, and he'd already forgotten.

"Short for Catherine, but everyone calls her Cat," I explained. "And get this, her last name is Lyon. She's practically one of us."

"No wonder she could hear you," Moony pointed out.

We spoke to bipeds all the time, but it was rare they listened. Cat was one of the good ones, as far as I could tell.

"I think she suspects the blonde lady with the big nose and behind," my brother conjectured.

"What makes you say that?" I didn't know much about her, but I thought she was called Karen.

"When Cat and her sidekick came out tonight to start cleaning, they were talking about her. Something like she lied about being sick, and she and the dead lady were mortal enemies."

"Mortal enemies? She said that?" I sharpened my claws on a nearby tree.

"Well, not in those words."

"What else?" I probed. Sometimes Moony had a bad habit of embellishing stories or leaving out important details—always one or the other. I needed to carefully steer the conversation so I could get the truth.

"She said the female was wearing a red shirt, and Cat also saw a flash of red at the front of the park right after we led them to the body. This female and the dead female didn't like each other. And she apparently lied about being sick. So…"

"Motive and opportunity," I filled in. I told you I watched a lot of detective shows.

"Um, sure," my brother agreed. "Anyway, they were talking about needing this piece of green paper that is in the trash can in the female's office. They said they need to sneak into her office later tonight to get it, but they aren't sure how they can pull it off."

I sat up tall and licked my lips. "They can leave that to us."

I WAS PROUD OF MYSELF FOR THE PLAN I CAME UP WITH. I gave the orders, and my cats came through. Ziti and Amber were stationed outside the building, where they got into one humdinger of a cat fight, complete with screeching, hissing, clawing and the works, which caused all the bipeds to come out to see what was going on, thereby leaving the door open for Moony and Ice to sneak inside. And the bipeds were so distracted by Ziti and Amber's antics, no one even noticed two cats wandering into the building.

Moony and Ice headed upstairs to the offices, and, by some miracle, Karen's office door was ajar. She was down the hall talking to Walter before he left for the day. Like a well-oiled machine, Ice stood guard while Moony slunk inside. He retrieved the green paper from the trash can, which he stuffed in his mouth, and the two paraded out a few minutes later when one of the other cleaning bipeds was heading out.

Next thing I knew, Moony was presenting me with the evidence of their triumph: the wadded-up paper. "I sure hope this is what they're looking for."

"It's green, isn't it?" Moony's whiskers twitched as he looked at me with narrowed eyes.

"Yes, but I'm sure there are other pieces of trash that are also green." I didn't put it back in my mouth—I didn't want to compromise the structural integrity of our prize. Instead, I batted it down the street like it was a ball of yarn or a mouse head or something.

Cat and her comrade rolled their carts toward the courtyard at the end of the street. I went into overtime, batting it back and forth with Moony like we were playing soccer (also frequently watched by some of the security personnel). We rolled it right up to Cat's feet.

"What's this?" She bent down to pick it up, gasping when she realized what it was.

She crouched down and looked me right in the eye. "How did you know?"

"We want to solve this murder too," I assured her. "We'll help any way we can."

And that was how we formed a partnership with the custodian biped and her animal print-wearing companion.

CATHERINE

I STARED AT ZOE AND HER ENTOURAGE in disbelief. Did they really retrieve the green memo form for me?

But before I could look at the wadded-up piece of paper, Gloria clutched my arm. "Is that what we were looking for?

I turned to face my coworker, the bottles of cleaning solution in my cart rattling softly in the midnight breeze. "Uh…yeah, so—" Was I going to have to explain the cats brought this to us on purpose? She'd never believe me.

She held up a hand. "You know what? Don't tell me. I don't need to know. I'm too old for nonsense, and it doesn't really matter. The point is, we have the clue we were looking for."

I was grateful she was letting me off the hook. "Yes! Let's see what it has to say." The paper was moist and somewhat pliable, which made me wonder what it had gone through to make it into my hands. I didn't want to know the answer to that, to be honest. Gloria had already proven ignorance was bliss, and I was gonna just go with that theory too.

The form I was holding, it turned out, had nothing to do with Karen at all.

It was actually a disciplinary write-up.

What?!

"Well, what does it say?" Gloria probed, unable to contain her curiosity.

I skimmed it, gulping when I got down to the bottom. "I

thought disciplinary forms were the marigold ones," I stated before wrapping my head around what I'd just read.

"They are," Gloria confirmed. "What does it say? Here, let me see it." She fished glasses out from a pocket in her tunic and settled them on her nose.

"Looks like Walter received a complaint from someone about her on day shift—sexual harassment!" I summarized.

"Why doesn't that surprise me?" Gloria shook her head and handed back the memo. "It looks like he used the green form to sweep it under the rug. But he did warn her—"

"If it happens again—" I rolled my eyes. It sounded like a hollow threat the way it was worded. It wasn't even a slap on the wrist. A green memo form wasn't going in anyone's personnel file. It was internal to our department.

"I wonder who made the complaint?" Gloria ventured. "He said he would write it up on the marigold form next time. And he made her sign the bottom of this form to acknowledge the warning."

She was right. That was the signature I'd seen when I spotted the form in Karen's office. "What was Karen doing with it? That's my question."

"Do you think there's any truth to this rumor something was going on between Heather and Walter?" Gloria questioned. We resumed rolling our carts toward the custodial building.

"That could explain why he didn't actually write her up." I turned to look at my friend. "I think we should talk to Karen again."

"Well, what are we gonna say, Cat?" Gloria stared at me, blinking. "That an actual cat dug the memo out of her trash and brought it to us?"

I shrugged. "Karen is weak. I think we could make her

believe we found it in the trash." I firmed up my plan. Our boss was naïve and not particularly assertive. We could work this to our advantage, and we could always threaten to go to Walter with our concerns.

If there was something our Goody-Two-Shoes Boss feared the most, it was getting into trouble—which was probably why she always put up with Heather's crap and never called her on it. She didn't want to get into trouble with Walter, or heaven forbid, the Forests.

"Follow my lead," I told Gloria.

My bestie smirked, but lights were dancing in her eyes as we rolled up to the offices.

Eight

CATHERINE

"You're still here." I knocked lightly on Karen's door and poked my head around the corner. Gloria was hot on my heels.

"Uh, of course I am. I work night shift too." Karen flashed us an uneasy smile after scrambling to tuck away a file that was open on her desk when I knocked.

"Can we come in for a sec? I wanted to ask you something." I kept my tone as light and nonconfrontational as I could. I wanted her to be relaxed. Wanted to get her talking.

She didn't like Heather—that much was already well known. If I could get her talking about Heather, something might slip. I'd been too forward, too in her face when I was in here earlier this evening. Now I had a better plan.

Gloria settled herself in the chair next to me, and Karen took a deep breath, as though steeling herself for an interrogation. That wouldn't do. I couldn't have her on the defensive.

"What's up?" She smiled and laced her fingers together on top of her desk.

"We were taking out the trash earlier, and something fell out on the ground. Gloria picked it up, and, I don't know, we were just curious if you knew anything about this." I handed her the wrinkled, crinkled memo, which I'd neatly folded into fourths.

Her eyes widened briefly as she recognized it, but she tried to play it off by clearing her throat and examining the evidence. "Huh, that's weird," she said after studying it for not really long enough to have read it for the first time. She clearly already knew what it said. "Looks like a memo from Walter to Heather about a complaint."

"Yes, that's what we surmised," Gloria chimed in.

"I wonder why it's a memo instead of a formal disciplinary write-up," I pressed. "You know, the marigold form instead of the green one."

Karen bit her lip. "Wow, that's a really good question. Maybe we should ask Walter?"

I flashed Gloria a look, and she shrugged. If Karen was the murderer, and this note had factored into her actions against Heather, I couldn't imagine she would want to confront Walter about it.

Honestly, I was surprised she'd want to confront him anyway. She was not a rock-the-boat kind of person. She seemed more like the type to let her rage boil up internally...until she wrapped her hands around someone's neck and didn't let go...

Oh. Right. That is *what happened.*

That was kind of how I imagined the Heather thing played out. Why her body was left in the middle of Storybook Street was another mystery for another day.

"Well, before we get Walter involved," I piped up, holding up a hand. "Do you know what this is about? Have you heard any gossip?"

She sank back into her desk chair, her face and upper chest area flushing slightly. She closed her eyes for a moment and let out a deep sigh that sounded downright weary. "I probably shouldn't tell you this," was how she chose to begin.

It took every ounce of my restraint not to rub my hands together in anticipation because she was about to spill the tea. *That's what the kids say these days, isn't it?* When I looked at Gloria out of the corner of my eye, her interest appeared similarly piqued.

Karen leaned in toward us. "You didn't hear it from me, but Walter and Heather have been…spotted together."

"Spotted?" My eyebrows arched as I searched for meaning on my boss's face. She was such a prude, I didn't know if she would really be forthcoming about the nature of their relationship.

She held her hands up, palms out. "Now, I don't claim to know if what I heard was true."

"Of course," both Gloria and I agreed, nodding.

"But many people claimed they saw Walter and Heather behind the building talking a few times. With no one around."

"Talking?"

"Yes. But they were alone," Karen clarified. "Unchaperoned."

"Unchaperoned," I repeated. What was this, the 1850s? It didn't really mean they were…intimate.

"Well, it's improper for them to be alone, outside…in the

dark…after hours," Karen claimed, grasping at her imaginary pearls. "But that's not the whole story…"

"It's not?" Gloria spoke up.

Karen shook her head. She had that kind of blonde hair that turned an almost platinum as it grayed, and her pale skin always looked somewhat afflicted with rosacea. But talking about this must have also embarrassed her, because she was flushed red as a lobster right now. I wasn't sure if that was a condemnation or an exoneration, to be honest.

"I overheard someone in HR talking about a…um… harassment complaint."

She couldn't even say the word "sexual." Wow.

"And, well, I'll be the first to admit Heather wasn't the easiest to get along with, not to mention the fact that I didn't agree with her…uh…life choices, we'll say. And knowing the rumors about her relationship with Walter, I wanted to know if she got written up."

"So did you get an answer to that question?"

"Well, yes. This form is the answer. He didn't put something in her personnel file. But—" She shook her head. "I'm sorry, this is hard for me. I don't like to speak ill of the dead. And I am terribly sorry about what happened to her, but there's been a lot of speculation over the years about her and her relationships with various male employees. The HR director was livid that she didn't get written up. I guess Heather stole her boyfriend a few years ago and—"

"Oh?" It was starting to look less and less like Karen was the suspect. I didn't think she would share all of this with us if she was trying to cover up a murder. But the HR director could be another possible suspect.

"Yes, it's well-known Ivy Ryan and Heather don't get along. It all goes back to Derek Swift in Security. Derek dumped Ivy about three years ago, and he and Heather were actually engaged for a while," Karen shared. Then she covered her face with her hands and shook her head. "I'm sorry, I really shouldn't be sharing all this with you. It's not professional at all."

I tried to set her mind at ease. "Don't worry about us, Karen. As far as we're concerned, there's a murder to solve, and we just want to get to the bottom of it so we—"

"Did you do it?" she blurted out.

What?!

I pointed my index finger at my own chest. "Me? Why would you think *I* did it?"

Her hands came back down to her desk, and she fumbled in one of the drawers, pulling out an antacid. She popped it in her mouth and took a swig from her water bottle, which was glittery blue with a silver "Jesus fish" emblem on it.

"It's another rumor circulating," she explained, "something about you and Heather getting into a fight after the meeting the other day. Plus, the detective asked me a ton of questions about your schedule, about your relationship with Heather, and then she implied Gloria might have been your accomplice."

"Oh, for heavens' sake!" Gloria cried. "You can't be serious right now."

Her voice quivered, "I'm so sorry. I've just been so upset about all of this, I can't sleep, can't eat. My stomach is in knots. I feel like, if we don't figure out who did it soon, they're going to—"

"Close the park," Gloria, Karen and I said in unison. "Longer than just one day," I added.

"Exactly," Karen said. "I can't imagine you doing something so heinous, but Heather had an effect on people…"

"Which was why we were asking what *you* knew," I confessed. "We know you fudged the time you left when you said you weren't feeling well. And you were wearing a red shirt. I saw a flash of red right about fifty yards away from her body."

"Me?!" Her jaw dropped. "You can't seriously think—"

"I don't think so anymore," I assured her. "But you've given us the idea to talk to Ivy in Human Resources. Do you think she would know who made the sexual harassment complaint?"

Karen shrugged. "It's possible. I'm glad you don't think I had something to do with it anymore. I just…I can't even wrap my head around how someone could be so cruel, so evil! And, for the record, I was wearing a red shirt—but I definitely wasn't here when Heather was killed. I did come back in after I clocked out, though. I left my Bible in my desk drawer."

She left her *Bible* in her desk drawer? *That* was her excuse? *Wow*. The innocent religious thing could very well be an act. But, no, it sounded like other folks had a stronger motive than Karen did. Also, the Jesus Fish water bottle had a friend: a leatherbound Bible sitting on the corner of Karen's desk.

"One more question," I said, and she lifted her chin in anticipation of it. "Did you and Heather fight in her office just before the toilet paper meeting?"

She shook her head. "No, I didn't even get in until minutes before the meeting. I came straight to the conference room."

"Okay. I just wondered. She was yelling at someone—but I couldn't figure out who. I didn't hear another voice," I said.

"Maybe it was Ivy? I know she talked to Heather—and probably Walter—about the harassment complaint."

I looked at Gloria. "Looks like we have some more investigating to do."

"And cleaning," Karen advised. "Don't forget your actual job."

"Right. That too."

ZOE

"Well, I've got some news, and you're not going to like it," Moony reported. He was accompanied by Ice, Cool, Amber and Ziti.

"Great." I glanced from face to face, waiting to see who was going to be charged with breaking the bad news to me. "Don't hold me in suspense."

Ziti stepped forward. "I talked to Vinny about what he saw the night of the murder. He was in the vicinity—actually near the park entrance."

"Right." I knew that, but he was completely standoffish when I confronted him about it. He really did not like me— probably because I was a threat to his masculinity. *These toms, I tell ya. So threatened by strong females.*

Ziti stretched her hind legs out before she resumed her seated position with her striped tail curled around her. "He said he would be willing to exchange information for a price."

"Did he actually see anything though? That's my question." I turned to the nearest tree and sharpened my claws, thinking about how I wouldn't mind sinking them into Vinny until he got over his major disrespect of me and my clowder.

"He claims to be able to describe the infamous 'biped in red' seen shortly after the murder," she revealed.

"Is that so?" My eyes narrowed. "And he would be willing to share that information in exchange for…what?"

A slick smile appeared on Moony's face as he stepped next to Ziti and sat beside her. She looked over at him, an adoring look on her face.

What's this? Does Ziti have a crush on my brother??? I filed that away for future reference.

"He was asking a few questions about the latest addition to our clowder," Moony revealed with the closest thing a cat's face can make to a smirk.

"Oh, he's interested in Priss, is he?" I rubbed my paws together. What was that saying about killing two birds with one stone?

"Princess," Ziti corrected.

"Scar is interested in her," Moony clarified.

"Now that's an interesting development…" My whiskers twitched as I licked my lips. "Guess I'll need to go have a talk with Vinny…"

Nine

CATHERINE

I was getting ready to clock out the next morning when I noticed a familiar tall, willowy figure wandering around the hallways of the custodial building. Detective Towers. Then her short, squat, balding sidekick came out of the men's restroom. Detective Powers. They were traveling as a pair today, apparently.

"How's the investigation going?" I approached them. Gloria had already gone home. She was extra tired after our shift, probably because we had to do a lot of special cleaning in the Hansel & Gretel's Great Escape ride.

"It's going," Shelly Towers answered. Her tone was so neutral, I couldn't get a feel about whether it was going well. "We're waiting on forensics," she clarified.

"And what brings you to our neck of the woods this morning?" I hadn't heard from the detective since I was summoned to her office, so I assumed I was no longer a suspect.

"You've worked here a long time, right?" She took a few steps closer to me, and her sidekick followed.

"You already know I have." I fought the eye roll. She had heard my life story at this point.

"We're looking for the murder weapon," she whispered.

"Um, okay?" I whispered back.

"Is there somewhere we can talk for a few minutes?" Her eyes darted all over the hallway.

I wasn't sure where everyone else was. My shift had ended, and most of the day shift custodians had reported, but they must have already been assigned. I wasn't sure who was supervising them now that Heather was gone, but whoever it was already had them busy. The park was reopening to the public at nine o'clock, and there was a lot to do.

"Yeah, we can probably duck into the lounge." I smiled and gestured down the hall to the open door on our right.

The three of us settled in, and Shelly whipped out her trusty yellow legal pad, which was full of inky scrawls by this point. I couldn't make out any of her notes, but I was wildly curious.

I wasn't going to tell her that my next suspect was in Human Resources or that I'd exonerated Karen. Why should I do their job for them?

"You were very helpful in giving us a background on the victim," Detective Towers pointed out, and her partner nodded in agreement. "We're still working on the video feeds of the parking lot and further down the main street of the park. You already know that the cameras that might have picked up the actual crime were turned off."

"That's what you said before," I noted.

"Right. Anyway, our medical examiner found that the

victim died of asphyxiation, likely caused by strangulation, and the ligature marks on her neck indicated the murder weapon was two to three inches in width."

"Wow, you can tell that by the mark on her neck?" I wondered aloud. I loved watching true crime type stuff, and forensics was fascinating to me. They had clues like this to go by on television shows and documentaries, but for some reason, I wasn't even thinking about that kind of clue in our case.

"Our case." I sounded like I was part of the detective team, didn't I?

Well, I seemed to be doing as good of job as they were, and I didn't have nearly the resources. I did have access to the park and all its employees though. That was a major advantage—plus knowing people's histories and relationships. I was in an ideal position to piece together the puzzle of Heather Suka's death.

"We can tell a lot of things from forensics," Detective Powers chimed in like he was just dying to be involved in the conversation. "We have plenty of leads—but having the murder weapon in hand, now that would really help solidify our case and possibly point to a suspect."

"Right." I nodded.

"Can you think of anything in the park…anything you've seen around that might have made that mark?" Detective Towers asked.

"Um…not off the top of my head, but I can certainly keep a lookout for something matching that description," I offered.

"Thank you. You already have my card. If you remember anything at all that might be helpful to our case, please don't hesitate to reach out," Shelly said.

"Of course. Not a problem."

They got up and left the lounge, saying hello to another figure who was entering at the same time. My eyes snapped to the doorway, falling on my boss, who looked frazzled.

"Walter, everything okay?" I stood up, noting how pale and waxy his skin looked.

He sighed and scrubbed his hands down his scalp and face, making the wispy orange hair on his head stand on end. "Those detectives make me nervous."

I laughed. "Why, do you have something to hide?"

"No, of course not. I just don't like them poking around here, and I don't like thinking that someone I work with could be a cold-blooded killer." He shuddered.

"I feel the same way." I walked over to the employee refrigerator and opened it, feeling the rush of cool air fan my skin. I needed to get home, but I also kind of wanted to talk to Walter for a bit, see if I could get anything out of him about that memo he'd made Heather sign.

He walked over to the counter. "I see Carol's cookies are already gone."

I laughed. "You know how much we love your wife's baking. I think she should bring cookies in every shift."

"I'll tell her you said that. It'll make her day." He smiled as he picked up the tray.

"Walter, is anything else going on that you'd like to talk about?" slipped out of my mouth before I could stop it. I hoped he didn't clam up. Maybe I could get him talking like I did Karen earlier.

He set the tray back down and turned to me. "I know all the rumors going around," he said. "About me and Heather…"

My eyebrow quirked as I stared at him, waiting for him

to finish his thought. I definitely did not want to disrupt him from sharing.

"Nothing happened between us," he insisted. "I know we were seen 'cavorting,' I think is the word I heard, behind the Guest Services building, but she took me out there because there was a little bunny that was injured. She thought one of the cats had gotten ahold of it."

Bunny? Cats? Hmmm…that I might need to verify with Zoe.

Still, I didn't say a word. Only listened.

"Well, she knew I'm a sucker for animals," he continued after a brief pause. "I came right over and…well, it was a setup."

"Setup?" This was getting crazier by the minute. "So there wasn't a baby bunny?"

"No." He chuckled a dark, humorless laugh. "I guess if you wanted to lure me into an unmarked white van, a sick or injured animal would be the way to do it."

This story had taken an interesting turn, one I hadn't expected. "What did she lure you into?"

"Turns out someone made a complaint about her—a sexual harassment complaint. She wanted me to sweep it under the rug. She put me in a compromising position so I would have to agree."

"Wow…" The green memo I'd seen earlier popped into my head.

"And…did you?"

"Sweep it under the rug?" He waited for me to nod. "Yes. I guess I did. But that opened another can of worms…"

"I see." I kind of knew the story from there, but this was making a lot of sense. I was connecting many dots.

"Heather had a lot of enemies here," he said, Captain Obvious style.

"I'm sure." I shook my head, remembering our conversation with Karen. "I didn't realize she had a son."

He nodded. "Yes, I've been in touch with him. Her funeral is on Friday. I know you're sleeping during the day, so I don't imagine you will go, but…but I feel I should be there."

"I understand. You were her boss." I smiled, wishing I could ease his obvious pain. He seemed to feel like he was responsible in some way for her death—as though by sweeping the complaint under the rug, it ticked off the wrong person, and that led to her demise.

I would have to figure out if that was the way things went down. And who filed the complaint against her.

ZOE

VINNY WAS LETTING OFF AN ODOR THAT MADE ME sick to my stomach—and he had marked his territory as well. I held my breath and gave Moony a resolute stare. My brother didn't want me to go alone, so he was by my side, and Ice and Cool were trailing a ways behind, planning to stay in the shadows while I had a chat with Scar's second.

"Can we talk for a moment?" I called over to the dense thicket where Scar and his gang ruled.

Vinny sauntered out just moments later, his own backup, Tony, a sleek gray shorthair, beside him. Vinny stopped to stretch then slowly made his way over to us like he couldn't be bothered to respect our time. He sat on his haunches, his tuxedo coat ruffled by the breeze coming in off the Ashley River.

"Whaddya want?" he practically hissed. "You don't belong here, Z." He never called me by my full name—only Z. He really made my coat crawl.

"I came to make a deal," I stated up front, because I didn't believe in wasting another cat's time or meaningless subterfuge. When I saw something I wanted, I went after it. And I wasn't going to stop now just because Vinny was a classless bully.

But I *was* going to use some artful deception to help my case. Some may even call it genius.

"You wanna make a deal with me?" He sized me up, brushing his long body against my fur as he stalked past me. His musky odor smacked me right in the face. *Gross.*

Moony was getting mad—his tail was violently swishing back and forth as he watched our interaction. A low growl rumbled in my brother's throat as Vinny made another pass at me. Tony looked like he was about to roll over in hysterical laughter at his captain's antics.

"I heard Scar was interested in our new girl," I said.

That stopped Vinny dead in his tracks. "Yeah, what about it?"

"Well, I might be agreeable to let her go...for a price." Before he could say anything else, I turned around and started to walk off, my tail waving proudly behind me. "Never mind—you aren't ready to negotiate."

"Wait, where ya goin', Z?" he called after me.

I whipped around. "You know what? It doesn't really matter. The info isn't that important to me. I've got other sources." I almost screwed up and told him I could communicate with the bipeds, but he'd only try to use that against me. I didn't want him to know that I had aligned with them. Only that I had other options.

"Oh yeah? But do you have eyewitnesses?" he practically purred.

"Yes," I lied. "And besides, Princess is assimilating very well into our clowder. She's so gorgeous, isn't she? I think she and Ice are starting to get along nicely, to tell you the truth."

I paced back and forth, enumerating Priss's finest qualities, all the while hoping Vinny would take the bait. He wasn't the sharpest claw on the paw, if you get my drift.

"Enough," Vinny said. "I already know she's special. She caught Scar's eye as soon as she arrived. He wants to arrange a meeting with her. If that goes well, we can further discuss your…ahem…proposition."

Grrr. I was hoping for a little more leverage.

Moony pawed his way over to me and rubbed his face against my cheek. "Don't give in so easily," he said under his breath.

"I'm afraid I can't promise anything without some collateral," I told Vinny. Tony came to sit next to him, the two of them striking a formidable presence silhouetted by the light coming from the Goblin Go-Karts attraction.

"Like what?" he spat back.

"Did you see a flash of red not far from where the dead body was found?" I blurted.

His nostrils flared slightly as he seemed to consider my bargain. "We did."

"Do you know who or what it was?" I questioned further.

Vinny looked at Tony, whose amber eyes just stared back, not revealing anything. "We don't have a positive ID just yet, but we are in the process of getting it."

"So you don't even know?" I fired at him.

The deal was off if they didn't have conclusive evidence. I wanted to take a name to Cat and her friend Gloria, help them out. We had the perfect partnership. She could navigate the biped world, and I could navigate and infiltrate spaces she could never access.

"I can tell you what I do know," he said. "And it should help narrow down the suspects."

"Okay, fine. Spill it, and I'll bring Princess over tomorrow night for Scar to meet."

"The biped fleeing right after the murder was female. Without a doubt female. And she had light-colored hair."

Ten

CATHERINE

I awoke to a voicemail message urging me to come into the park for a four o'clock meeting. Apparently the Forests insisted all employees attend one of three debriefing meetings with the owners, and the four o'clock one was the latest one. They were offering to pay overtime, so it was clear they were serious about this meeting. They never paid overtime willingly.

I found Gloria punching her timecard, and she shot me a wary look. "Why do I have a bad feeling about this?"

I shrugged. "Let's just hope the fact that they opened the park today is a good sign. And that this stays out of the media. Everyone's done an incredible job keeping it under wraps."

"Do you think they'll threaten us against speaking out?" Gloria questioned.

Jayden walked up to punch his timecard, clearly overhearing our conversation. "Geez, you guys really hate my family, don't you? They're not like that."

"No, we don't hate your family, Jay. Not at all. Your family has been very good to me through the years." I took a moment to collect my thoughts so I could deliver this as gently as possible to the naïve young adult standing in front of me. "Fairytale Forest is a business, though. And business owners have to make tough decisions sometimes—to protect themselves, to protect their business. When that happens, the employees often take the hit. That's all we're saying."

Jayden's brows crinkled. "I talked to my parents last night. They are absolutely devastated. My mom cried all day after she found out what happened to Heather."

I reached out and patted him on the shoulder. "I'm sure they're upset. Your parents are good people, Jay. Don't for a second think I don't appreciate everything they've done for me. I love my job, and their leadership and the culture they've created here are big reasons for that."

"Sorry I'm defensive." When he shook his head, the layers of his fine dark hair moved like fringe on a flapper's dress. "I don't know for sure what they plan to say in their convocation, but I don't think you have anything to worry about."

We both smiled at him then watched him go over to greet a few of the younger workers he'd become friends with this summer. He'd be starting classes at the College of Charleston this fall. I could remember when he was born, that was how long I'd worked here. I hoped he'd continue growing into a fine young man.

There was an auditorium at the very back of the Haunted Woods area of the park. There used to be a stage show years ago, but the Forests closed that attraction, and it had never been replaced. They used it to hold large staff meetings as there were nearly two thousand employees during the peak tourist season. So, Gloria and I had a bit of a walk ahead of us until Walter drove up beside us and offered us a ride in his golf cart.

We hopped aboard. "How are you doing?" I asked him as he drove down Storybook Street and onto the cobblestone courtyard that circled the tree.

"I'm okay." He didn't look at me as he spoke, just continued to steer the cart toward our destination.

"Do you have any idea what the meeting is about?" Gloria piped up from the back seat.

"Not really. They like to surprise managers at these things too." After driving around the tree, he took a wide path toward the creepy-looking black iron gates that delineated the Haunted Wood.

Most of the trees in the forest were live oaks and pines, and nearly all of them were filled with lush, trailing Spanish moss. The denseness of the trees coupled with the built-in aesthetics such as rundown shacks with broken windows, mysterious culverts, and huge hollowed-out logs that kids could crawl through created a creepy vibe that park visitors loved. A soundtrack with howls, creaks, whispers, and shrieks over scary music completed the effect, and at night, it was lit with LED lights.

We, along with a massive throng of fellow employees, poured into the auditorium, each finding seats in the audience section that surrounded the half-circle stage. An orchestra pit separated the seating from the stage area, and it was filled with boxes—some sort of ad hoc storage, I supposed.

The stage had several chairs set up, along with a podium. As we were getting settled, a group of park bigwigs and managers swarmed the stage, all chatting it up until Mr. Forest approached the microphone. Then they all scrambled for their respective seats. Walter, as Director of Facility Services, took one of the chairs. The Director of Human Resources took a seat next to him—Ivy Ryan. I didn't know her very well, but she was the one Karen implicated when we spoke with her.

Ivy was petite and slim, with dishwater-blonde hair and a curved nose that looked like the beak of a hawk. She crossed one leg over the other and laced her hands together on her knee as Mr. Forest, his wife at his side, adjusted the microphone for his height.

James Forest was a surprisingly short man, and I always forgot until I saw him in person. His wife, Janelle, was actually a bit taller than him, and she always wore flats. She was curvy and lovely with glossy dark wavy hair that always looked like it had just been professionally styled, and she had deep blue eyes that almost looked unreal. Maybe she wore colored contacts; I wasn't sure. She wore a classy navy-blue suit with a silk coral-colored blouse underneath. Her outfit contrasted nicely with her husband's khaki suit, crisp white shirt, and navy tie.

"Good afternoon, everyone, thank you for joining Janelle and me today to discuss the recent tragedy that has impacted our beloved Fairytale Forest." He cleared his throat, and the crowd of employees immediately silenced.

"I hate that we've been brought together today because we've lost a life—not just a life, but a member of our family. Heather Suka was the day shift custodial supervisor, and she'd been a part of our family for a long while.

We still do not know exactly how or why Heather left us—"

Hmm. I nudged Gloria, who flashed me a knowing look. We did know exactly how she "left" us. *That's quite the euphemism for being strangled, huh?*

"All we know is we must fully cooperate with law enforcement so we can answer these troubling questions and continue to make safety one of our core values here at Fairytale Forest. In the meantime, I know everyone was anxious to reopen today, and so far it looks like operations are going smoothly. Many of you are concerned about downtime and how this tragedy might impact operations going forward. Frankly, we don't expect operations to be affected beyond the closure yesterday."

There was a smattering of applause at that statement, which died out as people began to wonder if it was cold-hearted to clap in light of a fellow employee being dead and their killer on the loose.

"I know there are many other concerns related to this situation," James Forest continued. "One of which is specu-lation regarding who may have committed such a heinous act. The truth is there is no way of knowing at this time if it was another park employee, or if a guest stayed after hours in the park and either randomly or knowingly targeted the victim."

He was certainly dancing around the reality of the situa-tion, wasn't he?

"It's understandable there are some safety concerns surrounding the park, particularly for our second-shift personnel. Please be assured that police officers will be on the premises twenty-four-seven until the case is closed. And if you feel unsafe at any time, you can pick up any phone and dial 1-1-1 to reach our security team, who will be more than happy to assist with any issue you may be having, whether you have found something suspicious or want an escort to your vehicle or another part of the park. Please don't hesitate to contact them for any reason.

"If you see something, say something. That sounds trite, but it's one hundred percent mandatory at this time. The only way we are going to put this puzzle together and avoid any further issues is if we all work together to ensure safety and continuity of policies and procedures here in the park.

"Furthermore, if we want to go on serving the community with our much-loved and much-needed brand of family adventure, we must keep what has happened here to the confines of the park. Keeping the media out of our business is the way we move forward and keep the park open. You've all done an incredible job of adhering to the nondisclosure agreements you signed when you first began work. If you remember correctly, a clause specified that events that happen on premises are not to be discussed off-premises. This tragic event certainly qualifies. Of course, speaking with law enforcement is exempted, but our detectives and police are the only ones you should be sharing with. Is everyone clear?"

There were nods all around the room and a rumbling of affirmations.

"I want to thank you all for your continued good work and excellent service to Fairytale Forest. We could not operate this park without all of you, and I speak on behalf of Janelle and the entire Forest family when I tell you that we appreciate you all. God bless you, and God bless Fairytale Forest."

Mr. Forest always closed his speeches that way, and he liked us to repeat it back to him.

So we did, in unison: "God bless you, and God bless Fairytale Forest."

That meant we were dismissed.

I waited for everyone to filter offstage, and then I grabbed Gloria's hand and carved a path through the crowd to get to Ivy Ryan. "Hey, Ivy, can I chat with you a sec?"

The blonde blinked a few times as she studied my face. "I'm sorry, do I know you?"

We'd been introduced multiple times through the years, so there was no way she didn't know me. She was just being an elitist word-I-shouldn't-use.

I offered what I hoped was a gracious smile, extending my hand. "We've met before, but I'm Catherine Lyon from Custodial. My coworker Gloria and I are the ones who found Heather's body the other night. We have a few things we'd like to discuss with you. Will you be in your office after this?"

She looked hesitant, eyes darting around as though searching for an excuse. "I, uh, I guess so…"

"Do you mind if we stop by? We won't take up more than a few minutes of your time," I promised.

"Uh, okay…sure."

"Great, see you then!"

ZOE

Priss's plume of a tail waved in my face as she pranced away from me, unhappy with our conversation. Whatever. I wasn't looking to make a new friend. I had to do what was best for my clowder, and making her happy wasn't on the to-do list.

"What crawled up her butt?" my brother asked as he stumbled out of the bushes. "And aren't you awake kind of early?"

It was still afternoon in Fairytale Forest, but important clowder business needed to be done. Tonight was the arranged meeting between Scar and "Princess." And I just told the latter what her role was.

"She's mad that I'm making her work." I sighed. Being the leader was such a thankless job.

"Work? What do you mean? I thought you were just handing her over in exchange for the intel?" Ziti questioned. She'd slid out of the bushes—

Wait, were they in there together? *Hmmm.*

"You think I'm just going to send her over there with no strings attached?" I shook my head. "Use your brains, guys."

Moony scratched his head with his front paw. "Still don't get it."

"Priss didn't want to feel like a pawn, like she was just a piece of meat being thrown to the lions."

"Huh, that's one way to describe Scar and his feline mafia." Ziti chuckled.

"I wanted her to feel like she was serving a purpose, like she was important. You see, Priss needs to feel important. That's her whole MO, you know."

"That tracks," Moony agreed, crossing his one paw over the other and resting his belly on the grass.

"So I told her she's our spy, and that she is to report back to us all of the goings-on in Scar's little kingdom over there on the other side of the park."

"Do you think it will work?" Ziti tilted her head quizzically.

"Doesn't matter." I made bread against the soft grass, which felt so good under my paws. And I loved the sound of my claws catching in the roots—so satisfying. "If she does manage to bring back any intel, then bonus points, but the main objective is that she feels like she has a job to do."

"Why was she mad then?" Moony wondered.

"Because she's not used to working. She's been pampered her whole prissy life. Sat on a pedestal to be admired. Fed tasty treats in exchange for looking pretty," I explained.

"How did she ever end up here?" Ziti wanted to know.

"She was dumped here after her elderly owner passed," Cool relayed. He always knew these things—the tom had connections. "The son didn't want to take care of her."

"That's sad…" Ziti sniffled a bit.

"Poor girl." There wasn't any emotion behind Moony's words. And then he yawned so loud, I thought the bipeds surely must have heard him. "I should have slept longer…"

"Then go back to sleep. Your presence isn't necessary," I reminded him. I didn't say, "I'm doing all the work here anyway," but it was heartily implied.

"Fine." Moony's tail jerked as he pivoted and marched back to the bushes. Ziti followed him.

Those two had something cooking…

Eleven

CATHERINE

There was nothing cozy about Ivy's office. It was sleek, modern, and utilitarian, not a bit of softness anywhere. Even the plants were cacti. Prickly. Like her personality.

She sat stiffly behind her desk as we were ushered in by her administrative assistant, Gwen. "How may I help you ladies?"

"I'm concerned about Walter," I started out. I didn't adequately prepare for this, so I was flying by the seat of my pants.

My hastily formulated game plan was to stroke Ivy's ego and get her to talk. If there was one thing I'd learned about humans and psychology in my fifty-five years on the planet, it was that people loved to talk about themselves, be deferred to and revered as an expert on anything they felt was important.

"Walter McDuffy?" she questioned as though there were a dozen Walters running around the park.

"Um, yes. Director of Facility Management?" I tried not to sound patronizing, but…

Gloria's foot slid over and tapped mine as though she were issuing me another warning to watch my mouth. She did have a good feel for when I was about to cross a line.

"Why concerned?" Ivy pursed her lips and looked at something on her phone while she awaited my answer.

"He seems very stressed out about Heather's death," I began. "And I talked about it with my boss, Karen, and she was telling me some disturbing rumors that are circulating about Walter and Heather. I just—I'm worried about how this entire situation is affecting our department."

"Yes," Gloria chimed in. "It's creating somewhat of a toxic work environment. I'm sure you can understand."

We were both aware that "toxic work environment" was a phrase that made HR managers sit up and take notice. It was like the Batman signal for them. Hopefully she'd don her cape and swoop in to take the bait.

"What is it you'd like me to do about it?" Ivy laced her hands together, and I noticed her fingernails were long, red, and pointed. They looked like weapons.

Hmm. She wasn't *exactly* taking the bait.

"You could talk to Walter—see if he needs some professional help?" I suggested. "Actually, all of us who knew Heather should be offered free counseling. What happened to her is very upsetting. And it seems to really be impacting Walter."

Ivy scoffed. She actually scoffed at that!

"Look, Walter got into this mess on his own. He will be completely fine. I tried to tell him Heather Suka was someone to watch out for, but he's so gullible, he fell for her manipulation. Imagine racing down to rescue an injured bunny!" Ivy's head tilted back as laughter spilled from her throat.

Wow. Talk about insensitive. I thought, to work in Human Resources, you needed to be...you know, vaguely human.

I guess she was human. But she was not humane.

While I was scrambling for the right words, Gloria bailed me out. "Karen told us about the injured bunny. Why did Heather make that up?"

We already knew why—but it was smart of Gloria to ask so we could compare answers. And we'd find out if she was willing to share her own beef with Heather.

"Oh, Walter, you sweet summer child." Ivy shook her head, still laughing. "He fell for the oldest trick in the book. I mean, it's some real Regency Romance ish, you know? Trap a man, accuse him of impropriety if he doesn't do your bidding."

"Right, but what did Heather want him to do?" I probed. "She's gone now, so it shouldn't matter if you tell us. It might help us understand what he's going through. Maybe we can help him work through his feelings?"

"He needs to learn a lesson from this," Ivy continued. "He's far too trusting and loyal." She cleared her throat. "Heather, as you may have heard, was a...well, how should I put this delicately?" Her eyes gleamed as she plucked a word out of her mental vocabulary. "She was a real skank, you know?"

Gloria and I exchanged looks. "What does that have to do with Walter? He's a happily married man," Gloria expertly guided Ivy toward spilling the tea.

"Heather had gotten herself into a bit of a sticky spot—again," Ivy gloated. "You may have heard the rumors a few years ago that she stole my man."

I was surprised to hear her put it in those terms. I also did not miss the bitterness that dripped from them and hung in the air.

"She did? Girl, no one can steal your man," Gloria remarked. "If he thinks the grass is greener in another pasture, you best understand he'll be grazing in it before too long."

Gloria didn't mince words. One of the million reasons I loved her.

Ivy's nostrils flared as she carefully considered her next words. "Derek and I were perfectly happy until Heather started coming on to him at work. They dated for a while, and then she dumped him for her next conquest. She never did stay with them long."

"I'm sorry you went through that." I found empathy could go a long way. I wanted to keep her talking.

She sucked in a breath and lifted her chin. "Well, she probably did me a favor. Derek is a jerk. But apparently Heather didn't move on permanently because, a few weeks ago, she propositioned him. He reported her to Walter."

"Not to HR?" I questioned. "That would be the normal procedure, would it not?"

"Yes, he should have reported it to his supervisor, who would have helped him file a report with this office." She took an emery board out of her desk drawer and filed the nail of her index finger to an even sharper point. "But because of his prior relationship with me, you can imagine he didn't want to go through the proper channels. He didn't want me to tell him I told him so. I warned him she was crazy, but he didn't listen to me."

Interesting.

"So that was why she tried to manipulate Walter?" I ventured. So far this was matching up with Karen's story.

"Yes. She wanted him to sweep it under the rug so it didn't go into her file. You see, she has designs on a position in upper management."

"Had designs, you mean," I corrected her.

"Yes, that's what I mean. Sorry. It's still hard to believe she's gone." Ivy bit her lip and took another deep breath. "I think she really wanted to be *my* boss."

"Who is your boss now?" Gloria asked.

"The Director of Operations is who I report to," Ivy answered. "All the departmental directors report to him, including Walter. And he's retiring at the end of the year, so his position will be open."

"Are you applying for his job?" I didn't hesitate to ask.

"Why yes, I am."

Interesting. So, not only did she hate Heather because she "stole" her man, but she was also going to be competing against her for a promotion.

"So how did you find out about her little…dalliance with Walter?" was the next logical question.

Her eyes narrowed into thin slits as if she was remembering the circumstances. "Well, it didn't take long for the rumors to spread about him and Heather fooling around in the dark."

"I suppose not."

"I confronted Walter directly because I knew he wouldn't be unfaithful to his wife," Ivy explained. "That's when he told me about the injured bunny and the green-form memo he ended up agreeing to. He knew I was angry—and he knew why. We both agreed that if she continued to harass Derek, I would be writing her up, and it would be grounds for termination because there had been a previous complaint."

"Even though the green form said the next infraction would go in her employee file," I clarified. "Marigold form."

"What Walter did was against company policy. I could write him up too. He agreed with my course of action." Ivy sounded smug.

"Did you confront Heather yourself?" I continued my line of questioning.

It was funny because, at this point, I expected Ivy to be tight-lipped. I didn't think she would want to share anything further about the Heather situation, especially since they were enemies, and she had a perfectly understandable motive to harm her. But, for some reason, her mouth just kept moving, and her lips just kept flapping.

Gloria taught me a Gullah expression for someone who couldn't shut up: "E teet da dig e grave." It translated to, "Your teeth are going to dig your grave." And, looking over at my friend, I knew that sentiment was bouncing around in her head.

"Actually, yes. I did confront Heather," Ivy admitted.

A shock bolted through me as my eyes locked on hers. Her gaze was steady, unblinking as she said, "I told her a couple of days before her murder that I wouldn't tolerate her harassing any park employees or trying to get her slimy tentacles into any other men here. I reminded her that it was difficult for men to admit to being sexually harassed, but we were keeping an eye on her to make sure it didn't happen again."

"In other words, you weren't going to rely on the victims making reports," I gathered from her statement.

"That's right. Between all the cameras on premises and my eyes and ears in every department, I have a good idea of what happens here in Fairytale Forest." She sat back with another smug smile curling her lips.

"Then do *you* have any idea who murdered her?" Gloria asked before I had a chance to.

She sat up, her spine straight. "To be honest, I wouldn't be surprised if it was Derek. He had a violent streak. Ask me how I know."

Well, I wasn't going to venture that far, but the words "violent streak" caused a shudder to rack my body. We all sat there in silence for a few moments, while my heart pounded against my ribcage wondering what I should do or say next.

I still felt like Ivy's motive was as good as anyone else's— not that there weren't plenty of other folks on the Enemies of Heather Suka list. Was I brave enough to talk to Derek, though?

"You two should probably be heading out," she finally said, standing up and scooting her desk chair in. "I was supposed to leave twenty minutes ago, and aren't you two due to start your shift soon?"

We still had a while before our shift started, so I was thinking about a ride on the Little Red Riding Hood Coaster, but perhaps we'd see what other clues we could dig up first. As we were heading out, I noticed a sweater slung over Ivy's desk chair that I didn't notice when she was sitting in it.

It was a long red cable-knit cardigan with a matching two-inch-wide belt.

ZOE

"So you're gonna just leave her there with Scar?" Sass followed hot on my heels as I made my way back to the courtyard. I wanted to tell Cat what I'd found out about the mysterious figure in red: it was a female with light-colored hair.

"Well, how are they going to know if they like each other if they don't spend time together?" I said without looking back at her.

"Stop it, Zoe. This isn't like you. You're not usually so uncaring. Didn't you hear everything Princess went through before she came here?" Sass continued to whine.

My ears flew back. I stopped in my tracks and whirled around on my paws to face her. Daisy ran right into her when she stopped too, and they ended up an awkward tangle of tails and paws. *See what I have to deal with?*

I left Moony and the rest of the guys over by Scar's territory to keep an eye on Princess. I didn't like her, and I was a bit dubious about her tragic backstory, but I wasn't the monster Sass was making me out to be.

Once Sass and Daisy disentangled themselves, I tried to reason with them, though I doubted any degree of logic would permeate Daisy's two or three functioning brain cells. "Look, the park is in danger of being shut down if we don't figure out what happened to that biped and keep anything else like that from happening again," I explained. "I need Scar's cooperation, and Princess is actually doing us a very big service by helping us out. She has a chance to be the heroine in this story."

"What do you mean? You threw her to the wolves," Sass sputtered. "I mean cats!"

"Priss is stronger than you give her credit for." I made a circle around the two mollies and then went back to preening. I looked up to make my final comment on the matter: "She's going to gather some intel for us."

"Oh, she's a spy!" Sass finally got a clue.

"Shhh!" I shot her the stink-eye. "Scar has spies of his own, and they're everywhere."

"Why didn't you send me?" she purred. "I'd make a wonderful spy. And with my black fur, I can hide so easily."

She was only marginally smarter than Daisy, to be honest. "We're all cats, Sass. We can see you, even on the darkest night."

She pouted. "Fine, whatever. I'm gonna go find Moony."

Ziti and Amber rolled up as soon as she left. "I see you chased Sass away. Well done," Ziti praised. "Hey, Daisy."

"Hey." She laid there, looking comfy with her tail curled around her body. "Maybe I should go see what Sass is gonna do." She leaped up and took off with no further commentary. She always followed Sass around.

"Why didn't you send Sass instead?" Amber wondered. "You hate her."

"Keep your friends close, and your enemies closer. Haven't you ever heard that before?" Sheesh, these cats were dumb! Had they learned nothing from biped culture in all the years we'd lived here among them?

"Speaking of friends..." Ziti turned toward the courtyard at the familiar sound of rolling custodial carts. "Aren't those your biped friends?"

Yes! I'd been wanting to talk to Cat and Gloria. They had impeccable timing, as always. I supposed bipeds did have the advantage of watches and other time-keeping devices, whereas we had to rely on our innate internal clocks. Seemed unfair. Wouldn't I look stylish with a biped watch on one of my front paws?

"Well, look who it is!" Cat exclaimed. She abandoned her cart and approached us slowly, as though worried about scaring us off. Not like we were scared of her, but it was amusing that she thought we might be. Her friend stared at us from a distance, just smiling.

Cat crouched down near me, extending her hand. Was I supposed to sniff it? Was that what she was aiming for here?

Okay, fine, I sniffed her hand, which smelled like chemicals and flowers. Maybe a faint whiff of cheese. Then I rubbed up against her a little. Bipeds liked that, didn't they?

"Such a pretty girl," she cooed. "Listen, Gloria thinks I'm crazy, but you came through with the note from the trash, so let me ask you for another favor, okay?"

"Sure, what's up?" I answered her.

She jumped back a little, nearly landed on her bottom. "Oh, I can still understand you!" She seemed surprised and impressed. But she got over it quickly. "In the Guest Services building, there's a department called Human Resources. The person in charge of that department is named Ivy Ryan. She has a red sweater in her office with a belt. Do you know what a sweater and belt is?"

I sighed. "Yes, Cat. I don't wear clothes, but I am familiar with them."

"Perfect. Do you think you could get that belt for me? It could be the murder weapon..."

My eyes widened. "Really? You think this Ivy person did it? Does she have light hair?"

She blinked a few times. "Yes, she's blonde. If you can get me the belt, the police can probably run some tests on it to see if it was the object used to strangle Ms. Suka."

"Gotcha. I'm on it." I sat up tall and proud.

Cat headed over to her cart, chuckling under her breath about how it was so funny that she could communicate with cats. I didn't have the heart to tell her that anyone could if they tried hard enough. And if we wanted to cooperate, of course.

My species wasn't exactly known for being cooperative.

They walked away, heading toward the tree. Ziti looked up at me and frowned. "I thought you were supposed to tell them what Scar and Vinny said—"

Before I could chase them down, a catfight broke out in the bushes around the courtyard.

For meowing out loud, I couldn't get anything done tonight, could I? I'd have to go break up that fight before I did anything else.

Twelve

CATHERINE

"You heard what Ivy said," Gloria warned me. "She said Derek has a violent streak."

"But why would he hurt me? I just want to ask him a few questions. I've never even met him before. I mean, I know who he is, but—"

"I'm gonna go get started on the restrooms." Gloria raised her hands, palms up. "If you wanna talk to Derek, by all means, go ahead. But I'm gonna get to work."

Clearly, she didn't want to be involved in this part of my investigation. Fine. I could do this by myself, right? What was there to be scared of? He was just a man. And I'd be in the security office with a bunch of other security guards. They'd protect me if something went south, right?

"Okay, that's fine. Will you cover for me though? If Karen or Walter ask where I am?"

She sighed. "Yes, girl, you know I've always got your back."

I gave her a fist bump and listened to her cart roll away on the cobblestone. Sucking in a deep breath, I looked up at the looming tree. It was especially massive at night and up this close.

There were two security offices inside. One was in the first floor of the tree, and the other was at the very top—the control room with all the monitors. The lower offices were more for administrative purposes, and there was a staff lounge in there too. Neither was accessible without an employee badge. Beyond the newer rides, ID badges and readers were the most sophisticated tech in the entire park —and they'd just been installed a few years ago at security's insistence.

I didn't know if my badge would work to get into the lower offices, but I was going to try. I stepped up to the door, which was around back, out of sight of visitors. Holding my breath, I lifted the badge that hung from the lanyard around my neck and pressed it to the scanner. Imagine my surprise when it beeped, turned green, and an audible click of the lock disengaging sounded.

I'd never been inside the security offices before, and what I saw surprised me. You'd never know you were inside a huge tree. It was a state-of-the-art operation, boasting a sleek design and monitors covering most of the walls. One of them even showed me standing there awestruck.

"May I help you?" A pert blonde sat at the reception desk wearing a black polo shirt with the Fairytale Forest logo on the breast.

"Hi, um…is Derek Swift in tonight?" I thought he worked the night shift, which made me wonder how Heather could harass him if they weren't technically on the same shift. But maybe it was over the phone or online or something.

"He's in his office now, but he's due in the tower in twenty minutes," she said, looking at an electronic tablet in front of her. I was now starting to understand why we were all still stuck using green, goldenrod and salmon forms in the rest of the park. Security was taking the entire tech budget!

"This won't take long," I promised, though I had no idea how long it would take—or if he would even speak to me.

"May I tell him who is here to see him?" She looked up at me, blinking heavily lashed blue eyes.

"Uh, it's Catherine Lyon."

"And what may I tell him is the nature of your visit?" she inquired, still batting those eyelashes.

"Um…can you tell him it's about park security the night of the…murder?" I whispered the last word.

Her brow crinkled as she picked up a walkie-talkie and spoke into it. After a muffled response, she looked up at me. "He's in the third office on the left down this hall." She gestured behind the reception desk to a narrow, well-lit tunnel of a hallway that looked like it belonged on a spaceship.

I swallowed hard and nodded my thanks, then moved my trusty sneakers down the polished cement to the specified door. After knocking three times, I held my breath and waited.

"Come in," called a gruff voice that made me cringe.

"Hi, um, Derek. I'm Catherine Lyon," I introduced myself.

"Okay," was all he said. He looked back at the monitors in front of him. Each one was divided into four, so he was watching a grand total of twelve different views. I recognized all the areas of the park immediately.

"Do you mind if I sit down?" There was a chair next to his desk that I gestured to.

"Suit yourself," was all he said, never taking his eyes off the monitors.

"I can come back later, when you're on break, if you want." I didn't sit just yet, instead waiting for his answer.

He was a little younger than me, probably late forties, with dark hair that was graying at the temples, olive skin and possibly dark eyes, but I couldn't tell from this angle. He looked like he may have Italian heritage with his bushy eyebrows and his five o'clock shadow. He also had a prominent Adam's apple in a thick neck with broad shoulders and beefy arms.

I supposed he was attractive, if you were into the muscly Italian look.

Apparently Ivy and Heather both were.

"I can talk," he finally answered, "but I need to watch the screens. Mr. Forest was in here earlier today, practically ripped us all new you-know-whats. He wasn't happy about what happened here the other night."

"I imagine he wasn't," I sympathized then settled myself in the chair. Maybe I could get some answers out of him while he was distracted by the screens. "I heard the cameras on Storybook Street got turned off right before—"

"Yeah," he said. "Just the ones on the main street. And no one knows how it was done. Had to've been someone who knew what they were doing."

"So it definitely wasn't just a glitch?"

"Glitch?" He didn't look at me, but disbelief echoed in his tone. "These cameras have been running twenty-four-seven for years, and, yes, sometimes one will go out, but not eight at once."

"Eight cameras in total were turned off?"

"A whole sector," he confirmed. "The front main sector is what it's called. It covers from the end of Storybook Street to the park entrance."

"What about the parking lot?"

"Those were intact, but we've reviewed all the footage. The police reviewed all the footage. There's nothing other than the usual employees coming and going to their cars." His eyes very briefly darted over to me and then snapped right back to the monitors.

"What about Ivy Ryan?" I broached the topic.

He visibly flinched. "What about her?"

"Is she on the video…coming or going?"

"Not that I know of." Was he covering for her? He wasn't looking at me, so it was hard to get a read on if he was telling the truth.

"I understand you and Ivy were in a relationship," I shifted the conversation, suddenly feeling brave.

"That's right." His tone was clipped.

"But you left her for Heather…" Not a question, a statement.

"That's right." He slowly turned his head until his eyes stabbed into mine. "It was a long time ago."

"Is it true you filed a sexual harassment claim against Heather?"

Where was this audacity coming from? Though I'd always had a smart mouth and a lack of self-control, I didn't typically put my actual life in danger. I wasn't sure what had gotten into me, but I was highly motivated to solve this case.

"What, are you like a detective now or something?" he finally pushed back.

"I'm just trying to figure out if you have a motive." I looked around at all the monitors. "After all, you were here, and you had access to the security cameras. You could have turned them off. Maybe you were unhappy that Heather wasn't disciplined after you made the report against her."

"You have no idea what you're talking about, you know that?" His attention was definitely off the monitors now and fully on me. I'd clearly agitated him, and for some reason, it shot a thrill right through my heart.

"I'm piecing things together," I admitted. "I'm sure the police are too."

"I'd be careful if I were you," he gritted out between clenched teeth.

Ooooh…I'd struck a chord, clearly.

Then I heard something.

Was that a meow?

ZOE

HANK, WHO HAD BEEN CAMPED OUT under the bushes for the entirety of the evening thus far, was my witness when I came looking for Cat. "She went in the tree," he said with no hesitation whatsoever.

In my mouth, I was carrying a long red belt made of yarn. And something Moony found when he was doing his perimeter walk this evening. As soon as guests left the park, he made a sweep of the perimeter of our territory. He did it again in the morning before guests arrived. He'd picked up some sort of long, narrow tool and brought it to me, said I should show it to Cat. So now I was carrying both around like some sort of pack mule. The belt was dragging on the ground, and the wooden thingamabob was hurting my mouth.

"Tree, eh? Do you have any idea what she's doing in there? Cleaning?"

He shook his head, and his tail moved in time with it. "She didn't have her cart with her, or her sidekick."

"Do you mean Gloria?"

He yawned. Yes, lying around all day was extremely tiresome, wasn't it? "Yeah, whatever her name is."

I knew the security people. They knew me. I'd been going into that tree since I was a kitten. It had been a long time, but surely they'd be happy to see me?

I'd just go in there and track Cat down. Give her the item she requested and the bonus item Moony found. And I'd finish telling her what Scar and Vinny reported before I was so rudely interrupted by a catfight.

There was a tiny window in the security area on top of some sort of industrial air conditioning unit. I didn't know the technical term. I couldn't see in, but they could see out. If I jumped up there and tapped on the window, they would let me in. That used to be our system, anyway. We'd have to see if it still worked.

I couldn't exactly run over to the tree with all this stuff in my mouth, but I did my best to get there in a timely fashion. Jumping up on the unit also presented a challenge, but I rose to the occasion. I shook out my fur and pressed my paw against the window, letting my claws make a soft tapping sound.

A few minutes later, the door below swung open. *Victory!*

I hopped down and sashayed inside the security office, where all the bipeds oohed and awwed over my adorable furry self. It only took me a second to hear Cat's voice, and I took off down the hallway, a few curious bipeds following me to one of the cubicles, where she was speaking.

Ah. It was Derek's office. He wasn't my favorite biped, but he did like me.

"Zoe!" he exclaimed as soon as his eyes fell on me.

I offered him a meek "meow" in greeting.

Cat whipped around, her jaw dropping open when her eyes landed right on me. "Oh my!" Then her whole face brightened when she saw the belt in my mouth. I spit it and the wooden object out and sat proudly preening beside it.

"It's just one of the feral cats. They're responsible for keeping the park free of pests," Derek said—as if Cat didn't already know. As if Cat wasn't out in the park working her booty off every night. *Way to mansplain there, Derek. And, yes, I know what mansplaining is.*

"You don't say," Cat snarked back at him as she bent down and picked up the belt and the other item. She took another look at Derek, then glanced back at me. "Uh, thanks for your help. I've gotta go," she told him.

"You want me to follow you?" I asked her, knowing Derek wouldn't be able to understand me.

She smiled and nodded.

"Hey, you're not supposed to interact with the feral cats," Derek warned. "If they get too friendly with people, their handler takes them to a local shelter."

We both ignored Derek's sage advice and raced out of

the room. Following Cat, I ran down the hallway, happy to no longer be encumbered by the scavenger hunt items I'd handed over to her. With her coveted opposable thumbs, she was much better equipped for carrying stuff than I was. As a matter of fact, my jaw ached from carrying them, and I sure hoped I could find a decent meal tonight that didn't require too much effort. Frankly, I was feeling rather fatigued after all of this work.

The security folks said goodbye to me—presumably they were more interested in me than Cat—as we rushed back out into the humid night air. "Well, that's the belt you asked for," I said as soon as we were alone.

"Thanks, you did great," she praised me. "And what's with the knitting needle?"

"Oh, that's what that is?" I stared at her, blinking.

"Yeah, where did it come from?"

"Moony found it. He'd never seen anything like it before, and neither had I. We both thought it might be a weapon of some sort—but maybe not."

She shrugged. "Probably not, but I'll hang on to it anyway. It's a nice one."

"Need anything else?"

The rumble of a custodial cart interrupted us. Gloria was coming over to join us.

"Did you lose a knitting needle?" Cat asked her as she approached, holding up the one my brother found.

She took it out of Cat's hand and examined it. "No, but that's rosewood. It's an expensive needle." She handed it back and smiled. "I'm heading inside the main entrance to clean. You coming?"

Cat pulled out her phone and waved it. "Yeah, gotta make a quick call. Be right there."

Gloria smirked and rolled the cart to the other side of the tree, to the entrance park guests used to access the flying cars.

Once her friend was out of sight, Cat put away her phone and crouched down next to me. "Where did he find the knitting needle?"

"I'm not sure. I'll have to ask him." I heard a trill in the distance. "I've gotta go—we're having some clowder drama."

"Wow, okay. Have a good night." Cat waved to me as I scampered off toward the bushes where Hank was still dutifully stationed, part loaf, part sentinel.

Thirteen

CATHERINE

Dawn broke over the park as I was heading to clock out. Mauve and amber brushstrokes painted the wispy clouds that had gathered at the horizon to greet the rising sun. Soft golden light accentuated the trees adorned with trailing Spanish moss. The scent of pine and the marshy water floated on the air as I patted my crossbody purse, where I'd stashed the knit sweater belt and the knitting needle.

I doubted the latter had anything to do with Heather's murder, but it was a lovely rosewood needle. I always thought I'd take up knitting when I became a grandmother, but that didn't appear to be happening any time soon. Maybe I'd get a head start in case my sons ever decided to bless me with grandbabies.

Gloria had already left. She had a doctor's appointment in the afternoon, so she needed to get some sleep ahead of it. That was one thing I appreciated about the Forests, even if a lot of their policies and procedures were archaic. They were very good about giving time off. It was the best perk of the job.

My plan was to call Detective Towers and let her know my theory plus what I'd found. I still didn't think it was fair that I was doing the police's work for them, but maybe it would send good karma my way.

When I reached the custodial building, Detective Powers was there snooping around. "I was hoping to speak to you," he said, creeping up on me at the time clock like some sort of weirdo.

I shivered when his voice reached my ear, then I slowly turned around to face him. "Where's your boss?" I teased him.

He grimaced, clearly not appreciating my joke. "She's over in the administrative offices interviewing the Director of Human Resources."

"Ivy?" My eyebrows rose as I studied his waxy features.

He scrubbed a puffy hand down his shiny face. "I need to ask you a few questions about your boss."

"Karen?"

"And Walter." He nodded toward the table in the corner of the break room. It was the end of my shift, and the next would be beginning soon, so we were about to be inundated with people. There would be no privacy. I had a better plan.

"Actually, come with me. I know a better place." I took him down the hall to the big closet where we stored extra carts and supplies. It was doubtful anyone would need to get in there during shift change. And, if I remembered correctly, there was a stack of folding chairs in there for staff meetings.

I unlocked the door with an old-fashioned key—no

fancy-schmancy ID badge readers in here. It smelled like floor cleaner and Windex as I headed over to the stack of chairs. I lifted two down before the detective offered to help, and he took a seat without waiting for me to sit first. *So gentlemanly. Not.*

In that moment, I thought better of handing over the evidence I'd collected. I wanted to wait to hear what he said first. Also, I didn't know what his relationship was with his partner, but if it was adversarial, my loyalty was to her. You know, girl power and all. Something about this guy rubbed me the wrong way, and I wasn't going to make things too easy on him.

"Tell me what you know about your boss's vendetta against the victim." He took out a mini yellow legal pad, poised to scribble, before looking up to meet my gaze.

"Well, Karen and Heather didn't get along," I confirmed. "The issue went back to when Karen worked in Dining Services and used to complain about Heather's workers not getting things clean enough."

He scribbled on the pad. "Is that all?"

"Isn't that enough?" I joked. "But seriously, I don't think Karen did it. Besides, I already covered all this with Shelly."

"Why don't you think Karen did it?" One corner of his lip twisted down.

"I've known Karen for a while now, and she's pretty religious. Not to say that a religious person isn't capable of murder, but she's—well, she's a bit…prissy to put her hands around someone's neck and strangle them."

"But did you know she lied about her whereabouts the night of the murder?" the detective continued. "And that a witness saw a flash of red not that far from where the body was found, and Ms. York was wearing a red shirt that night."

"Yes." I rolled my eyes. "I am aware because I *am* that witness. I'm also the one who noticed she didn't leave when she said she did." Sheesh! This guy was tap dancing on my very last nerve. "But you should look at Ivy Ryan a little more closely. She has a much bigger beef with Heather."

"She does?"

"Yes, besides the fact that Heather stole her man, she was angry that Heather went behind her back to address a disciplinary issue when Ivy should have been involved—"

I could tell the detective was unimpressed and about to say, "So?"

"…and they were both up for the same promotion. Ivy didn't think Heather should get it since she'd been accused of sexual harassment, but the report didn't go into Heather's personnel file because she worked out a deal with her boss to give her a mild warning instead. And, by the way, the person who made the report is the same man Heather stole from Ivy a few years ago: Derek Swift. Look him up—he works in Security."

Detective Powers scratched his chin. "I see. And you know all of this how?"

"I've worked here a long time, Detective. I have developed a good rapport with most of my coworkers and superiors. People like to tell me things. And I have a good knack for telling when someone is lying."

I did, didn't I? I didn't usually toot my own horn, but I might be in a better position to investigate this crime than he was.

"There you guys are," a female voice sounded at the door. I nearly jumped out of my chair. It was Detective Towers. "I've been looking all over for you."

"Oh, I was looking for you too." I stood up. "Detective

Powers and I were just discussing the case, specifically what Ivy Ryan and Derek Swift have to do with it."

"I just spoke to Karen York," Shelly Towers said. "She filled me in."

"Good. You should talk to Ivy too. I was in her office yesterday afternoon, and I found something you may be interested in…" I reached into my purse and pulled out the long red knit belt.

Detective Towers audibly gasped, and a thrill shot through me. "Where did you get that?"

"I went to talk to Ivy about the sexual harassment complaint Derek Swift filed against Heather, but Walter covered for her so it wouldn't go in her permanent file. Right when I got up to leave her office, I noticed she had a red sweater draped over her desk chair. And guess what was in said sweater?" I held up the belt. "Didn't you say the murder weapon was two inches or so wide?"

"Why, yes. Yes I did." Her eyes were bright with excitement as she took the belt from me. "If she was wearing that sweater the night of the crime, then she could have easily pulled the belt through the loops and wrapped it around Heather's neck."

"Exactly," I stated. "And Derek could have shut off the cameras for her."

"Now who's Derek?" They were both taking notes.

I sighed. "Did Karen tell you about how Heather stole her boyfriend from her?"

Shelly nodded.

"So, his name is Derek Swift, and he's the one who filed the complaint against Heather. When I talked to Ivy, she said I should speak to Derek—but that he had a violent streak." I puffed up my chest. "He told me eight cameras were turned off that night. He called it the front main sector."

"You've really done your homework!" Detective Towers sounded impressed. At least someone did their homework, right? "Hey, maybe if you get tired of the custodial gig, you could come work for the Charleston PD?" She laughed.

And leave Gloria, the cats, and my beloved trash? Never!

ZOE

"Scar is asking to speak with you," Moony reported at our evening check-in.

I yawned, then lifted my paw to give it a lick and nibble.

"Well, are you going to respond?" my brother pressed.

"Tell him I'm busy tonight but maybe tomorrow night."

"He said he found something and wants to show it to you," Moony said.

I sighed.

Yes, cats can sigh. Don't get it twisted—we may seem aloof and unemotional, but we have plenty of thoughts and feelings running through the brains in our beautiful, sleek, nature's-perfect-killing-machine bodies at any given time. Yes, most of these thoughts involve ways to murder small rodents—or possibly each other—but they're there.

"Do I have to do everything around here?" I stretched my back, feeling the satisfying burn in my limbs as my brother awaited a proper answer. While I stalled, my clowder gathered around me: Hank, in loaf form, had been here all along; Ice, Cool, Amber, and Ziti now dotted the landscape around me. Daisy wandered in looking like she'd just woken up, her fluffy tail jerking behind her.

"Where's Sass?" I glanced around, waiting for her lithe black figure to slink out of the shadows that were gathering as dusk gave way to night. The crowds in the park the last day since it reopened had been enormous. I could sense it was going to be a very good hunting night indeed.

"She went to talk to Princess," Ziti piped up.

"She's not supposed to do that without permission from me," I seethed, looking from face to face. They were all aware of how unwise it was to anger me. "Again, do I have to do everything around here?"

"You're the one who wanted to be in charge," Moony reminded me.

"Silence!" I hissed.

Once all I could hear were the frogs down by the river and the custodians sweeping the cobblestone on the court-yard, I was able to get my mind to function. "Fine. We'll go see Scar. I'd like to have a word with that traitor, Sass, anyway."

"He said to meet him at the edge of the Haunted Wood." Moony shuddered as he said it. He was scared of the Haunted Woods. To be fair, it was the creepiest place in the park—hence the name. But I loved it. The creepier the better. I really should have been an all-black cat, but I got gray fur instead. Go figure.

"Fine. We're taking a field trip to the Haunted Wood, everyone." I tried to gather up my troops, but it was, as you might imagine, like herding cats.

Moony was flirting with Ziti. Hank was still in loaf

form. And Daisy had started to chase a cricket into the bushes.

This was my life. Surrounded by incompetence.

We trudged onward, reaching the Haunted Wood in record time—*record for the slowest time, that is.* Vinny was waiting at the rusted iron gates that separated this area from the rest of the park. It wasn't their territory, but the clowder that lived in the woods was, well, weird. They were disorganized and didn't have a real leader. Was this where they housed new arrivals until they joined more formal clowders? Why they didn't put Princess there in the first place was anyone's best guess. I was sure it had to do with her pedigree.

Anyhoo…I sashayed right up to Vinny. "What's up?"

"We wanted you to see something, Z." He didn't hesitate at all, and he looked a little anxious, ears back, eyes darting around to check for danger. He was supposed to be a tough guy…so I wasn't sure what had spooked him, other than just being in the Haunted Woods, of course.

We all squeezed through the bars of the fence that separated the Haunted Wood from the rest of the park. Except Hank—he couldn't fit. But he didn't seem to mind. He'd pounced on a dropped hot dog and was basically in kitty heaven.

"Over here." There was urgency in Vinny's voice as he trotted away in the lead. We all followed. I thought they were going to try to give Princess back to us—I wasn't expecting there to be a real thing for us to see.

He stopped at the edge of the woods, where the twisted trees and branches formed an eerie tunnel over the path. "Do you see that?" His head tilted to the forest, and I blinked as it came into focus.

A long red piece of yarn was tangled through the underlying brush, looking like a web woven by an absolutely massive spider. "This isn't part of the park, right? Not a new attraction?"

"No, the Miss Muffet display is on the other side of the woods," Vinny explained. "This just appeared overnight. And you found a knitting needle?"

"We did," I confirmed. There was either a mole among us or he had spies. Either way, I wasn't happy. I only wanted the intel to flow from them to us, not the other way around.

"Red yarn." I went over to it and took a sniff. There was a faint scent of coconut and florals like a woman's perfume or hand lotion. "Any idea how it got like this?"

"Yeah, the clowder over here was playing with a whole ball of yarn—a real big one," he said. "I guess they batted it into the bushes. Not sure where the ball came from though."

"I'm surprised the park maintenance people haven't removed it," I commented, walking from one end of the bush to the other, where the yarn began.

Vinny paced back and forth in front of the bush as he answered, "They don't come over here much. There's nothing over here to clean, just a few statues for photo ops."

He was right. We were at the front of the Haunted Woods, and you had to go down the path a ways before the actual exhibits began, which were just plain weird. Bipeds liked being scared. I always found that strange.

"Where do you think the yarn came from?" he asked.

"A biped," I answered without a second thought. "Duh."

"Right, but—"

"Why are you so freaked out about this?" My green eyes met his amber ones.

He sat up taller, showing off his "bowtie." He had tuxedo

markings with a splotch of black under his chin that looked like a bowtie. You could only see it if he was sitting up tall with his head lifted. "I'm not freaked out," he insisted.

But his eyes darted around the woods before landing back on me, calling him out on his lie.

"Fine," he hissed. "I heard that bipeds who kill other bipeds sometimes get their start killing animals." He choked out, "Especially cats."

"Oh, you're thinking of serial killers!" If I had fingers, I would have snapped them as I made the connection. I remembered watching some documentaries about them when I used to spend time with the security bipeds.

"Cereal killers?" His stark white whiskers contrasted against the black markings on his face when he shook his head. "They like to eat Cheerios and Frosted Flakes?"

"No," I practically roared with laughter (for a cat, that means my lips twitched slightly with amusement), "a *serial* killer. It's spelled differently, I think. It's not like I know how to read, but one of the bipeds made a joke about it once. Anyway, they're weirdos who kill multiple bipeds, often somewhat randomly, or bipeds who meet a certain set of criteria. That's not the same thing as the murder in our park. This one was motivated by absolute rage and loathing. You know, *justifiable* reasons."

"Loathing?"

"Yeah, pure hatred," I explained. Vinny didn't have a very extensive vocabulary, obviously.

He relaxed just a little. "Do you think the yarn has something to do with the killer?"

"It's possible," I said. "Let me talk to the biped I'm working with to solve this crime. And let me know if you see anything else suspicious, okay?"

He nodded then leaned forward, hope gleaming in his eyes. "While you're here…would you consider taking Princess back? She never shuts up, I swear. Scar is already tired of her. And so are the rest of us."

"Hmm, that sounds like a you problem to me." I gave him a slight smirk and scampered off toward where my clowder was waiting for me.

Red ball of yarn. Interesting. Maybe the red sweater belt I spent so much effort stealing and carrying all over the park didn't have anything to do with the murder after all… but this red ball of yarn might.

Fourteen

CATHERINE

I was starting to hate the sound of my phone ringing instead of my alarm. It was never good news—either a telemarketer, some sort of scam, or something to do with this murder.

Today was no different.

"Hello?" I grumbled into the phone.

"Did I wake you up?"

"Who is this?" I yawned.

"It's Karen. Have you seen the news?"

"No, I don't own a television." Books are a thing, ya know? And I could never justify paying for cable since I worked all night and slept during the day. I only had a few hours of me-time, and I preferred to spend it reading.

"Well, the press has gotten wind of the story," she said, breathless. "And they closed the park."

My heart immediately attempted a swan dive right out

of my chest. I couldn't conceal a gasp either. "For how long?"

"I don't know," Karen answered. "But I heard the Forests are considering hiring a private investigator. Rumor is they're not too happy with the way the police have handled it."

Probably because the only leads they had were ones I'd given them, and so far they hadn't exactly led in a definitive direction. I wondered if they'd questioned Derek yet. Or examined the sweater belt I gave them.

I returned my focus to my boss as the realization dawned on me. "So I have the day off then?"

"I guess we all do." She sighed wistfully. "Hopefully the shutdown won't last long. Mr. Forest is just worried that guests will boycott the park until the murder is solved and the perp is behind bars."

"Makes sense. That's why we were trying to keep it under wraps." I swung my legs over the side of the bed and planted my feet on the floor.

My phone buzzed with a notification of a text coming in from an unfamiliar number. If people were going to keep bothering me, there was a zero percent chance I would be able to go back to sleep—even if I did have a serendipitous day off. Once my brain woke up, there was no way I could settle myself back down again, and my engines were now firing on all cylinders.

"I'll let you know if I hear more," Karen promised. She was being a lot nicer to me since we had that heart-to-heart about Heather's write-up in her office.

"Thanks, Karen. Talk to ya later."

I hung up and switched over to my text messages. Very few people texted me—basically only my sons. Gloria said she didn't trust this "new-fangled" communication process. "If I wanna talk to y'all, I'll call y'all up like a civilized person," she always said. So I had no clue who may be trying to reach me.

I definitely didn't have what happened next on my bingo card.

> Unknown number: Hi, it's Jayden Forest. My parents heard you've been helping the police with the investigation. They'd like to meet with you.

My heart kicked up a thunderous beat. I didn't know whether to be honored or scared out of my wits that the Fairytale Forest theme park owners wanted to speak with me about my efforts to get to the bottom of the murder. And I really hoped it wasn't some sort of trap—like the detectives still thought I had something to do with Heather's death, and they were luring me in to arrest me.

Why did my mind always immediately snap to the worst-case scenario?

I took a deep breath and composed a message to Jayden in my head before attempting a real reply on my phone.

> Me: How did you get this number?

It wasn't much of an answer, but it would buy me some time to strategize.

> Jayden: From the employee database. Can you come to my parents' house?

Me: When? Where?

Jayden: 21 King Street. As soon as you can.

That street was well-known. It was in the Charleston Historic District, just a block or two away from the Battery. I couldn't even imagine how much that house was worth. I absolutely adored the old houses in that part of town—I'd always fantasized about owning one myself. I should go just to see the inside of it. I was sure I'd walked past it a hundred times, though I couldn't place exactly which one it was by memory alone.

Me: I'll be there in an hour.

MY NISSAN ROGUE LOOKED TERRIBLY OUT OF PLACE NEAR the BMWs and Mercedes parked along King Street in the historic downtown area. Nevertheless, I found a spot not too far from 21 King Street. The three-story mansions loomed into the sky on either side of the narrow street, which was lined with oak trees, their boughs decorated with Spanish moss.

The Forests' home was an Italianate style with a tri-level porch and balcony on the left side. Stepping up to the porch, which was filled with beautiful planters holding glossy dark-leaved ivy and understated white blooms, the first thing I noticed in the arched doorway was an owl statue perched so it looked down at the massive wooden door. Holding my breath, I pushed the doorbell.

I shouldn't have been surprised that a plump middle-aged white woman with her hair in a silver-streaked bun, wearing a crisp, starched gray and white maids' uniform, answered the door. "Good afternoon," she greeted me. "Are you Catherine Lyon? The Forests are expecting you."

I smiled and nodded, following her into the impressive hallway, my eyes darting from floor to ceiling. The former was fashioned from warm amber-colored wood dotted with immaculate Persian rugs, and the latter were pristine, with impossibly ornate trims and mouldings. Chandeliers dripping with elegant crystal baubles lit up the passage from the foyer to the rest of the first floor.

"You may wait in here," she said. "I'm Margaret. Would you like some tea or coffee? The Forests will be right in."

"Coffee would be wonderful." I chose a striped settee, admiring the looming oil portraits staring at me as I tried to make myself comfortable. I'd chosen one of my dressier outfits—a floral skirt and a silk shell under a lightweight mint-colored cardigan—but I still felt underdressed in this formal space.

Margaret poured me a delicate floral teacup full of coffee and set it beside me in a matching saucer. Both the cup and saucer were rimmed with gold. She handed me a cloth napkin and said, "Make yourself at home." Then she scurried out, her soft shoes making no sound on the wood floors.

Ha, as if I could ever feel at home in this space. My fantasy of owning one of the houses in the historic district was quickly mired by thoughts of maintenance and cleaning. I was the custodian at a theme park. Of course I could guess exactly how much work went into keeping a place of this size and magnitude spotless. I hoped Margaret had some help.

I sipped the coffee, and it nearly scalded my tongue. I set it back down, carefully avoiding any spillage, just as the door creaked open. Mr. and Mrs. Forest came into view.

They were a stylish couple in their early fifties, so right around my age. Mrs. Forest, Janelle, looked as though she'd had some work done. Glossy dark waves bounced around her shoulders. Her face glowed, and her minimal makeup was expertly applied. I wondered if she had someone who did it for her. She was wearing a sleeveless flax-colored linen shift dress with a navy and white scarf and navy sandals.

Mr. Forest, looking more relaxed than usual, wore khaki pants and a navy polo. I stood up as he approached, reaching me in two strides with his hand outstretched. "Ms. Lyon, thank you so much for coming on such short notice."

"Mr. Forest, Mrs. Forest, hello. I'm happy to help however I can," I answered as his firm grip nearly crushed my hand. "Please, call me Catherine or Cat."

I noticed he did not ask me to call them James and Janelle. Oh, well. The couple seated themselves on the loveseat across from me, and Mrs. Forest nodded to Margaret, who once again scurried from the room.

I folded my hands in my lap and waited for one of them to speak.

Mrs. Forest cleared her throat. "We really do appreciate you driving down here. I know traffic and parking can be a pain. We wanted to pick your brain about what happened at the park a few nights ago. I know you spoke with the detectives. Shelly said you turned in something you believed may have been the…um…" She apparently couldn't bring herself to say "murder weapon." It was a much-too-gruesome phrase to form on her lips.

"Murder weapon," Mr. Forest jumped in on her behalf. But he didn't appear fazed. "They said they were looking for something a little wider. Do you have any more leads?"

Wow, he certainly cut to the chase, did he not? I was immensely bummed that Ivy's sweater belt was not it, but I'd been plagued by a persistent lingering doubt.

"I, uh…well, I'm not a detective or anything," I spoke carefully. "It's not my place to get involved, but I…well, I couldn't help noticing a few details. And, of course, I didn't want the park to be closed down. So anything I can do to help get it reopened, naturally, I'm willing to do. Do you have any idea how it got leaked to the press?"

Mr. and Mrs. Forest exchanged a worried glance before they both turned their gazes to me. Mrs. Forest deferred to her husband. "We're not entirely sure, we think it might have come from the police."

"Wow…" I'd heard they had an in with the cops, but I didn't know the real story. I was surprised it stayed out of the media for as long as it did, to be honest. It was a race against time to solve the crime before it was broadcast all over South Carolina—a race we had apparently lost.

"Well, it's too late to do anything about it now," Mrs. Forest said, straightening her spine and lifting her chin. "We just have to move forward at this point."

"Which is why we asked you here," Mr. Forest's gray-green eyes landed on me. They were full of fear—and hope.

I had something they wanted—not a position I ever thought I'd find myself in with the owners of the company I worked for. I had never even really met them before today —only saw them in passing at meetings and holiday func-tions. I would have never dreamed in a million years they'd invite me to their multi-million-dollar home in the historic district. They did know I was just a janitor, right?

"Like I said, I'll help however I can." I swallowed hard, waiting for their big ask.

"We know you're not a professional," Mrs. Forest began, "but you do know the park and its employees well. And you have a way about you, a way of interacting with people that puts them at ease, makes them comfortable sharing information."

"I do?" I blinked rapidly, wondering who had told them these things about me.

"You work with our son Jayden," Mr. Forest reminded me. "And you worked with his older brother and sister before him. Our children hold you in the highest regard."

Blood was pumping so hard through my body that all I could hear was it rushing through my ears, which were burning hot with a mixture of surprise and embarrassment. I wasn't used to receiving accolades, especially not from someone as rich and powerful as James Forest.

"All we're asking is that you be extra observant. If you see something…hear something…say something," Mrs. Forest followed up. "Share it with us and with the detectives. Let's keep the lines of communication open and solve this…crime…before any more damage is done."

My jaw firmed as my gaze darted between both of them. "I'll do my best. You have my word."

ZOE

I was sure something bad was going on. I woke up from my afternoon snooze, and there were no bipeds anywhere. Because our clowder was so centrally located, there were always bipeds around, even in the middle of the night.

I didn't get very far before Moony was in my face. "Did you hear?" my brother asked.

"Hear what?"

"They closed the park. Police are combing it for evidence. We need to stay out of sight," he warned.

"The police won't hurt us." I leaned forward and stretched, feeling the burn in my neck and legs. "They know we're here."

"Scar sent Vinny over to negotiate about Princess," was the next tidbit my brother shared with me.

Can't a cat wake up to some good news once in a while? Grrrr. "I already told him we didn't want her back," I hissed. "Where are they?"

"Over near the tree. The park is closed, but security is still here. And the police." Moony paced back and forth like he was patrolling the bushes.

I yawned and stretched again for good measure. Maybe I'd wake up for real, and things wouldn't suck. "I wonder if I can find out anything from them. Do you know if Cat is here? Or her sidekick, Gloria?"

"I think they gave the cleaning bipeds the day off. Haven't seen any of them," he reported.

"Drat. I wanted to tell her about the ball of yarn. She said something about knitting hooks? Don't bipeds use those and yarn to make stuff, like that sweater I had to steal the belt from?"

"I do think it's amusing that bipeds have to wear clothes since they don't have fur like we do." Moony strutted around in a circle, his tail waving proudly.

Now that I was awake—and reality was settling in—I took a closer look at him. "Why is your fur matted behind your ears?"

"I got into it with Vinny and his thugs—about Princess. I told him you weren't going to take her back. Are you going to go meet with them or what?"

"I told you not to fight with them," I chastised my brother. "They're not worth it. Bunch of low-life scum. I can't believe we have to cooperate with them because of this stupid murder."

He stopped right in front of me. "I still don't understand why you think we do."

"All of us cats need to stick together." I started to head toward the tree, and he followed right on my tail. "If we don't get this murder solved, the park is going to stay closed, and they might get rid of us. Do you want to be rounded up and shipped off to some tiny apartment in the city or something? Or do you want to have a whole park to roam freely and chase your dinner like a civilized feline?"

"Well, I don't want to be stuck in an apartment, but being fed posh canned food every night doesn't sound half bad." He licked his lips.

"You have no idea, Moony. It's not worth it. Trust me." I looked to the sky, smelling Vinny's foul odor on the breeze. "Give me liberty, or give me death. I think a famous biped said that a while back."

We arrived at the tree, and in its shadow was Vinny and a couple of his goons. Alfie was a fat short-haired gray cat, and Bruce was a rare male tortoiseshell. For some reason, that gave him a really bad attitude. Or maybe he'd just been hanging out with Scar and Vinny for too long. I was surprised to see they didn't even have Princess with them.

"What did you do with her?" was my first question. I didn't like her, but I didn't want any harm to come to her either.

Vinny had some wounds around his ears that I noticed as I grew closer. Looked like Moony had gotten him good. "Where's Princess?" I reiterated.

"Your brother won that round," Vinny practically spat at me. "But it's not over yet."

My hackles rose, and my ears flicked back. "I said, where is she?" There was plenty of authority in my voice. Vinny and his goons didn't scare me.

"Relax, Z. She's back in the Haunted Wood with Sass. I promised your brother I wouldn't try to pawn her off on you guys—today. All bets are off tomorrow." His tail twitched menacingly.

"Look, if this murder doesn't get solved *pronto allegro*, there's not gonna be too many more tomorrows here in the park," I warned him. "In case you didn't notice, they closed the gates today. No customers, no rodents, no money—no need for cat exterminators."

"Yeah, that's why I'm here." He sat up straight, his nostrils flaring as his thugs came to sit on either side of him like two ugly gargoyles. *Huh, that's redundant, isn't it?*

I was losing patience with this dolt. "Well, give it to me then. What happened?"

"Remember that yarn in the bushes in the Haunted Wood?"

"Yeah?"

"Well, the police came and took it," he said, stepping

toward me. "They stood around looking at it from every which angle, and then they stuffed it in a big plastic bag and took off with it."

"Gotcha. Well, that's a good thing." My nostrils flared as his stench intensified.

"Is it?" He drew even closer, his amber eyes mere slits.

"Yeah, maybe it will help them solve the case." I hated to back away, but I needed a pure, unadulterated breath of air.

"By the way," he seethed, "we know the real reason you sent us Princess and won't take her back."

They didn't know their tails from a snake in the grass.

"Retribution is coming." He scowled at me, his ears nearly flat against his head and his tail flicking back and forth like a whip. He lifted one paw and waved his sharp claws at me. "This is your one and only warning."

Fifteen

CATHERINE

One thing I got from the Forests when I visited their home in the Charleston Historic District was unfettered access to the park. In exchange for my help, they rendered my ID badge somewhat of a golden key, and even though it meant going to work on my day off, I was excited about being able to nose around the place.

I drove straight from their house on King Street over to the park and slid my Nissan Rogue into one of the VIP employee spots at the very front. I felt even more special when I buzzed myself in the front gates.

It felt totally different than my usual arrivals because Storybook Street wasn't full of park guests. And when I looked up at the offices on the second and third floors of the Guest Services building, the windows were dark. That meant Walter, Karen, Ivy et cetera were not here.

I made my way toward the tree, thinking about how liberating it was to walk without pushing a cart. I called Gloria on the way here to tell her what was up. Snippets of the conversation were still floating in my head:

"You went to their HOUSE?!" She was flabbergasted. "On King Street? Lord, I don't reckon I'll ever get that invite. Do you think a Gullah person has been in that house since the Civil War ended?"

"It was just as ostentatious on the inside as you might imagine," I informed her. "How many chandeliers does one house need?"

"That's what I wanna know!" She laughed a deep chuckle. "How long do y'all think this closure is gonna last?"

"They didn't say. But they want me to poke around. They gave me basically a golden key to the whole place." I couldn't contain my excitement.

"Who woulda ever thought one of us custodians would be valued for more than pushing a mop?" A wistful sigh sounded over the line. "You sure you don't want me to come and help you?"

I thought about it for a hot minute. I loved Gloria's company. I truly loved the woman with all my heart. But she would slow me down. And I wanted to find Zoe and have a talk with her—I didn't exactly want to do that with Gloria looking on thinking I was off my rocker.

Though, maybe now that I'd caught up on sleep a bit, I wouldn't hear the cats talking to me anymore. Well, actually, it was just Zoe I heard. I wasn't able to hear the other ones, though perhaps they just hadn't spoken to me yet?

I was still more than a little weirded out by the whole thing, but we'd reached a critical juncture: if we didn't get a murder suspect arrested in a jiffy, the park was going to be closed for the foreseeable future, and that meant I'd lose my livelihood. At fifty-five years of age, I didn't relish the thought of finding a new job. Who was going to hire a washed-up custodian who'd only ever worked at one place?

I headed straight for the courtyard. That was where Zoe and her crew hung out, and I wanted to know if she'd found anything else. But before I could search for the cats, a familiar face lit up when they saw me. It was Detective Towers, heading out of the security entrance of the tree and making a beeline right to me.

"Oh, Cathy!" she said, her voice much higher and shriller than I remembered. *Also, have I mentioned how much I hate being called Cathy? It makes me cringe.*

"Can I help you with something, Detective?" I tried to put on a pleasant face, but with the way the sun was glaring, I probably looked squinty and scowly.

"I wanted to touch base with you about the Forests." She smiled as if I had leveled up a bit. I was clearly on a higher rung of the ladder now that the Forests had requested my help.

"Yes?" I blinked a few times. My smile just wasn't cooperating—my whole mouth was protesting to go back into frown mode.

"Mr. Forest told me he's given you access to the entire park so you can collect some information. I just want to be sure you know you're to share any and all information you collect with myself and Detective Powers." Her voice was firm, but she was also maintaining what looked to be a forced smile.

"Of course. Were you able to interview Derek Swift?" I tilted my head toward the tree. "I spoke with him the other night, and he was telling me eight cameras in total were turned off. The front main sector." I was fairly sure I'd already given her this information.

"Mr. Swift has an alibi for the evening," she explained.

"Are you sure? He didn't say anything to me about not being there the night of the murder. And I was also told he has a violent streak. He has motive too—he filed a complaint against Heather, and—"

"He was at his mother's funeral," Detective Towers shared.

"Are you sure?" I sighed. I hadn't heard anything about that. I thought the Forests usually sent out company-wide emails whenever someone was on bereavement leave. They always sent a planter to the funeral home as well.

"Yes. I examined the death certificate and can confirm he was not at the park that day or night. Apparently she was from a big Italian family. Mr. Swift flew to Long Island to attend the funeral and returned the day after Ms. Suka was murdered."

Huh, I thought he looked Italian. At least I was right about that.

"What about Ivy Ryan then? She and Heather were up for the same promotion, and Heather stole Derek from her," I remembered. "You said the sweater belt wasn't the murder weapon, but that doesn't mean she couldn't have used something else."

Detective Towers shook her head. "Ivy also had an alibi that night. She was teaching yoga, then went back to her home and was in bed by ten o'clock. Her Ring camera corroborates this."

Shoot. Another theory foiled. "So where does that leave us?"

"Well," Shelly's face brightened, "the sweater belt was a good theory, but the medical examiner says the actual width of the ligature mark was 2.75 inches—a little wider than the sweater belt. So we're still looking for that."

Grumble, grumble. I was riding quite the roller coaster today, and it wasn't a ride at the park. I'd had the high of receiving my "golden key" and now the crushing defeat of my suspects being ruled out. Maybe the detective would throw me a bone. "Okay. Do you have any other leads?"

"We are reviewing Ms. Suka's personnel file today and looking at all the employees she had direct contact with, then cross-referencing that with the ones who have access to the security cameras," she stated.

I crossed my arms over my chest. "That makes sense. Well, how many people is that?"

"Not very many," she confirmed. "Mr. Swift was one. There are three others."

"Care to provide some names?" Why didn't this information sharing work both ways? It should be a two-way street.

"We'll let you know what we find out, if it's relevant," Shelly insisted. "But I did want to ask you something else."

"Fine." I wrapped my arms around my body, feeling a bitter wind kick up. It looked like it was going to storm at any moment. Layers and layers of thick gray clouds were moving in, setting low toward the horizon, just over the treetops.

"Do you know anything about a ball of red yarn?" she asked.

"Red yarn?" *Hmm.* Rosewood knitting needle, yes, but I didn't know anything about yarn. The knitting needle was in my car, but I wasn't about to bring it up since I didn't turn it over to her when it was first found. "I don't think so. Why?"

"The feral cats that take care of the park were playing with a ball of yarn in the woods there behind the tree." She pointed in the direction of The Haunted Woods. "It was wrapped around some bushes."

"Okay?" That was surely just a coincidence. Probably didn't have anything to do with the knitting needle. And even if it did—there were plenty of women in my age group employed at the park. I bet we had several knitters on staff. Heck, Gloria was a knitter, come to think of it.

Her gaze stabbed into me. "Do you knit?"

"Well, bless your heart, no, I do not knit." I was *this close* to losing my patience with her. "Look, haven't I already been exonerated?" This was making me madder than a wet hen!

She sighed. "Yeah, I suppose so."

"Fine. Well, y'all're gonna have to figure something else out. Because I'm one hundred percent innocent, and I've been *trying* to help y'all out!" There was no way to hide my exasperation now. The Southern-fried was coming out.

"Be on the lookout for knitters," she said.

"Yeah, will do."

ZOE

I camped out in the bushes waiting for Cat to finish talking to the female police biped, who was so gangly that her front legs and back legs were almost the same length. I almost expected her to lower to all fours and scamper off like a monkey.

But I was glad to see Cat was finally alone because I wanted to have a word with her. I didn't think she would be here today since the park was closed, but it was a pleasant surprise that she'd shown up. I never thought I'd feel anything resembling affection toward a biped, but Cat had earned my trust. And we both had a vested interest in finding the killer and getting the park back to status quo.

I didn't want anyone to see us communicating, so I hoped to get her attention and ask her to meet me somewhere more private. She was a smart cookie—spotting me in the bushes as soon as she ended her conversation.

She walked away from the other female murmuring, "Yeah, that should be no problem. There are only one or two knitters here, after all," and rolling her eyes like bipeds did when they thought something was completely ridiculous.

"Zoe," she gasped when she saw me. "Let's find someplace to chat."

I sat up straight, my tail a silver plume behind me slowly twitching back and forth. "The castle," was all I said. The Princess and the Pea castle was set off a bit from the main part of the park, and its towering façade would provide some cover.

She smiled and nodded. "Meet you there," she whispered.

I watched her roam off in that direction, and I summoned my posse: Moony, Ice, Ziti and Amber. I didn't know where Sass or Daisy had gotten off to, and Cool looked exhausted. I'd left him asleep in the bushes, and I wanted him to stay there and rest. If he got wind of a potential adventure, he'd be too excited to sleep and insist on joining in. Hank was, naturally, asleep too, curled up in a big round orange ball that was nearly impermeable to sight, sound, smell, or reason.

We got ready to leave, and Moony suddenly stopped and sniffed the air like a dog. We all ground to a halt, and I looked back over my shoulder at him. "Is there a problem?"

"I heard Sass scream," he said. "Didn't you?"

I looked at Ice, Ziti, and Amber, and they shook their heads. "We didn't hear anything."

"Something's wrong. I'm gonna go check it out. I'll meet you at the castle."

"Fine, be careful," I warned him.

Four sets of paws sprang off the grass as we raced toward the castle. Looking around when we arrived, I smugly reveled in our victory—we'd beaten Cat. There she was, coming up the slight hill—there weren't really hills in the Lowcountry of South Carolina, and this one was clearly biped-made.

The glittery pink castle was a walk-through exhibit that little biped females liked. They generally dressed in flowing gowns and wore sparkling tiaras on their heads, and they threw big wailing fits when they didn't get their way. The castle wasn't really as big as it looked—there were some clever design features that made it appear to tower into the sky, but it was actually dwarfed by the enormous tree in the center of the park. The castle sat on the banks of a small tributary of the Ashley River that wound its way through the park. On the other side of it was the Water Fairy boat ride, which the little females also adored.

The largest concentration of tiny princesses was always

in this area of the park, so it was one I generally avoided at all costs. But with the park closed…well, I could see how nice it was over here. Especially without the ear-piercing shrieks, whines, and giggles of little bipeds.

Cat walked across the drawbridge spanning the moat, which was connected to the aforementioned tributary. She turned around with a gleeful smile when the badge she wore around her neck unlocked the front entrance to the castle, marked by a pair of heavy wood doors decorated with stained glass and brass fixtures.

"Hey, look at that, it works!" she exclaimed as she marched inside, gesturing for us to follow her.

Here in the cavernous castle, we were alone. I didn't see any evidence of other bipeds.

Cat glanced around the perimeter of the room, ostensibly looking for cameras. "I'm hoping they're turned off, but we should try to avoid them anyway—just in case." She gave a satisfied nod when she walked into a smaller room off the main hallway. Once again, the badge hanging around her neck buzzed and allowed us entrance.

"Janitors' closet," she explained, and we were greeted by the strong scent of cleaners and shelving units full of paper products, supplies, and cleaning implements. Bipeds were certainly obsessed with cleanliness. Though, I supposed cats were too. We spent a great portion of our time cleaning ourselves, after all.

"Okay, so we are sort of back at square one," she announced. "Ivy, Derek, and Karen have all been cleared."

Cat looked stressed. I didn't typically care about bipeds' feelings, but her stress was kind of bleeding into my own emotions. Or maybe we were both just stressed for the same reason: the park being closed. We could survive a day or two of closure. But what would happen if it stayed closed for a week…a month…while the bungling detectives wasted time and still didn't capture the culprit?

We'd all be out of jobs.

The park owners? The upper management? Those were the richest bipeds. I knew enough from watching all those shows with the security folks when I was a kitten that rich bipeds didn't have to worry about work. They always had options.

It was always the less fortunate who were hit harder.

And I supposed our entire cat colony was among the less fortunate in this scenario. We'd all be adopted out, given away, split up. And we'd have absolutely no say in what became of us.

Before I could think of anything to say to Cat, we all heard the skittering of paws on the floors, and suddenly Moony and Sass appeared, their hackles raised and their eyes gleaming with fear.

"What in the wild whiskers happened to you?" I demanded as they slid to a stop right beside me. Moony was carrying a piece of paper in his mouth.

Sass was out of breath, but she still looked to be in better shape than my brother. I was surprised to see her, to be honest. "Scar put a hit out on Moony," she panted.

"WHAT?!" I shrieked.

Cat shook her head. "What's going on? I can only under-stand you, Zoe."

I lifted a paw to Cat before turning back to my brother. "What's in your mouth, and what the frack is going on?"

He spit out the piece of paper, and Cat automatically bent to pick it up. I ignored that for the time being—I wanted a straight answer out of this fool sitting in front of me.

"He made Scar really mad," Sass supplied.

"Moony, what happened?" I redirected the conversation to him. I didn't want to hear Sass's version. I wanted to hear my brother's.

He gulped down some air, his tail twitching nervously as he fought to bring his breathing under control. "Sorry, we ran all the way from Scar's territory. They caught Sass communicating with Princess, and…and I don't know what they did with her. They dragged her off somewhere, and they tried to take Sass too. I stood up to Vinny and his thugs again, just like I did the other day. Well, Scar got involved. And let's just say, he's not happy with me. Especially since I stole this from him." He lifted his chin toward the piece of paper Cat was now examining.

"What is it?" I asked her. "And why would Scar care about it?"

She turned it over and read the back side, the furrow between her brows deepening the more she read. "It's a knitting pattern," she said as if completely blown away with shock.

"A knitting pattern," I repeated. "Why on earth would Scar care about that?"

"He said it was related to the ball of yarn they found," Moony explained. "He just wanted to keep it from us so we couldn't help the bipeds."

Cat obviously couldn't understand him, but she murmured, "Maybe it has something to do with the knitting needle you found and that ball of yarn I just learned about. The detective told me to be on the lookout for a knitter."

"Well, that helps, right?" I blinked a few times, hoping to see her lips turn up in a more hopeful expression.

"Not really," she said. "There are a lot of knitters at the park, including my friend Gloria. This pattern is for a baby blanket. Do you know how many grandmas work at this park? This is gonna be like finding a needle in a haystack. And I'm still not convinced these clues have anything at all to do with Heather Suka's murder."

Sixteen

CATHERINE

I stood there with a semi-circle of cats around me. I could only understand Zoe, but there appeared to be an issue with the gray and white long-haired tom we called Moony and the sleek, lithe black female known as Sass. They came racing in with a piece of paper that Moony spit out, and I picked up.

It was a knitting pattern, specifically a pattern for a baby blanket. What was up with all this knitting stuff? A lot of employees knitted, but why was all this knitting paraphernalia turning up now?

Surely the murderer wasn't a knitter. These clues had to be red herrings, right? Clues planted to throw us off the scent of the real killer.

Before I could delve into the whole psychological landmine of the fact that I could hear one of the cats talking, I decided to think hard about who had the most to gain from

Heather's death. I was making this too complicated with all these clues and chasing suspects.

It all came down to motive, means, and opportunity, right? *Keep it simple, stupid.* I'd start with who had the greatest motive.

Think, think, think! I admonished myself as I walked back toward the center of the park. Zoe and her crew had rushed off toward The Krakken seafood restaurant, no doubt looking for some leftovers. I was positive there was a different group of cats who lived in that area, but maybe they were friends. I still didn't understand what was going on with Zoe's black short-hair and gray-and-white longhair friends. I promised her I'd come find her tomorrow.

Hopefully the park would be open.

As I headed toward the front, my eyes scanning every nook and cranny for any overlooked clues, my phone rang. It was Gloria.

"Hey, lady, did you get to sleep in today?" I questioned when her raspy voice greeted me.

"You know I did, my friend. But I am none too happy about this park closure. I wondered if you might wanna grab some dinner in Mount Pleasant and talk it over?" There was a sense of urgency in her voice that wasn't usually there.

Gloria lived in Mount Pleasant, which was a lovely community on the other side of the Cooper River. I'd get to cross the beautiful Ravenel Bridge and have dinner with my bestie. Didn't sound like a bad idea at all. "Where did you have in mind?"

She rattled off a few suggestions, and I decided one of the restaurants on Shem Creek would be lovely. "I'm going to run home and change clothes, and I'll meet you there."

She agreed, and I hung up. Right before I was getting ready to leave the park, I ran into Walter, who looked rather out of sorts.

"What's wrong?" I asked, surveying his disheveled appearance. "Why didn't you get the day off?"

He wrung his hands, working hard to focus on me. "Forest wanted all the managers here for a meeting. I'm getting ready to head up to his office at the top of the tree."

"Don't be nervous. I'm sure you are all getting paid whether the park is open or not, right?" I smiled and patted him gently on the shoulder. I wasn't usually the touchy-feely type, but he looked like he needed some sort of reassurance.

"I just don't like what's going on. I feel bad that my employee got murdered...at work. Like it was my job to protect her." His volume faded as though he couldn't believe he was admitting it to me.

"I know you and Heather had a history," I said, "but surely no one thinks you were responsible for her death or could have prevented it."

He swallowed hard. "I regret not taking Derek's complaint straight to HR. She conned me." He sighed. I was surprised he assumed I knew the story.

He continued, "I guess she had a way of doing that to people. She was a narcissist—that's what my wife says. Carol has tried to help absolve me of any misplaced guilt, but...I'm just not built that way." He forced a smile. "Being a manager is hard sometimes."

"I'm sure. I definitely couldn't do it," I assured him.

His graying brows arched. "You don't think so?"

I shook my head.

"You know what, Cat? I think you could. I think you'd be

really good at it, in fact." He looked down at his watch. "Well, I better get going. The meeting starts soon, and I still have to get there."

"Hopefully I'll see you back at work soon." I smiled at him and watched him hurry away in the lumbering, plodding way he had.

Walter was a stand-up guy. He didn't deserve to be in the middle of this mess. It made me even angrier that Heather chose to get him involved. I needed to find the murderer for Walter too.

ZOE

AFTER MY CONVERSATION WITH CAT, I decided we should take advantage of being out in the daytime to do some hunting. Some delicious treats preferred foraging in the daylight hours, and this was the best time to catch them unaware. But we struck out at The Krakken, so we all split up to maximize our chances of catching dinner.

I cornered a small but nevertheless juicy rat on my way back to the courtyard. It was nosing around a trashcan outside the Hansel and Gretel ride. After my snack, I licked my lips and continued on, keeping my eyes and ears peeled for anything of relevance to the investigation or to my stomach—which was a bit rumbly and could do with a nice dessert.

I was almost to the tree when I heard a shriek that sent a

chill down my spine. I raced toward the bushes where Ziti and Amber were watching, eyes wide in horror.

I bounded over to join them. "What's wrong?"

Ziti's whole body shook as she filled me in. "Look across the courtyard on the other side of the tree. The handler and some other bipeds have Moony cornered!"

"What?!" I started to march out of the bushes toward where my brother was being lured into a trap, but my loyal mollies pulled me back.

"No!" Amber insisted. "They'll take you too."

"What happened? Why are they taking him? Where are they taking him?" The questions were flying out of my mouth so fast, I was getting spit all over my whiskers.

"He pissed Scar off," was all Ziti would say. "So they set him up."

"What do you mean? How did they set him up? Where's Ice? Where's Cool?" I needed more information.

I watched as my brother was locked into the carrier. The handler picked it up and headed toward the front of the park.

I wanted to run after him, but Mr. Cool Cat appeared out of nowhere and blocked my path. He shook his head solemnly but didn't say a word.

My heart sank. I needed answers, and I needed them fast. And then I needed to get my brother back.

MY REMAINING CLOWDER GATHERED AROUND ME AS TWILIGHT descended upon the park. The moon rose in the sky, partially veiled by gauzy clouds as stars began to twinkle through the branches of the towering tree in the center of the courtyard.

"I'm just... I don't even know what to say right now," I admitted to my fellow felines. Moony may have been the only one of them blood-related to me, but I considered all of them to be my family.

They looked at me, empathy shining in their eyes—well, as much empathy as cats can muster up, which is a relatively small amount. But they weren't used to me being rendered speechless. And I wasn't used to feeling helpless and hopeless.

"He shouldn't have been messing with Scar," Ice maintained. He scratched his hindquarters before his long pink tongue stroked up his leg.

"Can you not do that there?" I requested before he spread his legs and waged a full-scale tongue-bath on his privates. "I don't want to see that right now, okay? I'm traumatized enough as it is."

"Sorry..." He sat up, tail twitching back and forth. "Still...Moony shouldn't have let his temper get the better of him."

Hank sat up on his haunches—it was rare to see him out of loaf form. "I miss Moony already."

"Why is Scar such a scumbag?" Amber wanted to know.

"He's always been that way," Sass said, prowling out of the bush across the courtyard and slinking in our direction. "Trust me, we go way back."

"You're one of his spies," Ice accused her. "So I don't know why we'd listen to you."

Sass arched her back and glared at Ice. "While it's true I used to report some things to Vinny, I lost all respect for him and Scar when they treated Princess so horribly."

I leaned in closer. "They were annoyed by her, sure, but what exactly have they done to her?"

"They're holding her captive in a tiny area, barely giving her enough food to keep her alive." Sass said it nonchalantly, but by the way her tail whipped back and forth, I could tell she was disturbed by it.

"Why did no one tell me this?" I demanded.

"You didn't want to hear it," Sass answered. "You were so insistent on getting rid of her—"

"Well, she was annoying," Ziti agreed. But she changed the subject immediately. "We have to get Moony back."

"I'm going to talk to Cat as soon as I can," I promised everyone. "Hopefully tomorrow. I had my doubts about befriending a biped, but I think it's going to pay off."

"Can we trust her though?" Amber questioned.

"She's one of the good ones," Cool interjected. "She's been around as long as I can remember, and I've been here forever."

"I'll just have to ask her for help." I swallowed hard. Asking for help wasn't one of my strong suits. But I would do anything to be reunited with my brother.

Seventeen

The view of the sun setting over Shem Creek was breathtaking as Gloria and I settled into a cozy booth in one of the most laid-back seafood restaurants in Mt. Pleasant. We both perused our menus quickly to choose our orders so we could get straight to the gossip and not be interrupted when the server came by.

"Got it," she said, closing her menu and setting it on the table. "So out with it. What's going on?"

"Well, I went to the park today after the Forests asked me to keep investigating."

"And…?"

"Well, the detectives think we should be looking for a knitter. And after the clue I found today, I'm starting to wonder."

"A knitter?" Gloria's finely arched brow quirked even higher. "Like someone who knits?"

I blinked three times fast. "Yes, um, what did you think I said?"

"Never mind about that. Why, I knit. So do half of the ladies we work with!" She gave an unimpressed sigh.

I laughed. "Exactly. It doesn't exactly narrow things down. We have to come at this from a different angle."

"Good. I was hoping you weren't putting me in the hot seat." Gloria laughed and stirred her sweet tea that the server set down before he whipped out his order pad.

She ordered stuffed shrimp, and I ordered shrimp and grits. We were both going home with full, happy bellies tonight!

"We need to figure out who has the most to gain from Heather being dead," I announced, possibly a little too loudly, as one of the ladies at the table next to us gave us a long, hard glare. We both laughed, of course.

"Well, the list is long and distinguished," Gloria finally said when the smoke cleared.

"We already crossed Karen, Derek and Ivy off the list. So who else are we missing?" Heather had a lot of enemies, but who would hate her enough to kill her?

"Well…Ivy told us about the promotion she was up for. Who else might have been vying for it? Operations manager —that would be a pretty big step up for anyone in a middle management position," Gloria pointed out.

"What about the Director of Security?" I ventured.

"Rory Blake?" Gloria questioned.

I nodded. "And it would explain how the cameras got turned off…"

Gloria scratched her chin. "Good point. Now, did he know Heather? Did they have any type of relationship?"

"I'll have to ask around." I took a sip of my water as

Gloria sipped her sweet tea. A million thoughts were buzzing in our minds like bees around a hive. We just needed those thoughts to coalesce and make us some honey.

I wanted to tell Gloria about the strange encounter I had with the cats today at the castle, but I was afraid she might think I was crazy. I wasn't completely convinced I wasn't crazy either, for that matter.

"Do you think they'll open the park up tomorrow?" She took the silverware out of her napkin and laid it across her lap. She was wearing a vibrant royal-blue tunic today with zebra-print leggings. Her head was wrapped in a multi-colored cloth that brought the focus to her wise brown eyes.

"I doubt it. I really don't think they'll open it until there's a suspect behind bars. Mr. and Mrs. Forest are supposed to do a press conference tomorrow… That reminds me. I ran into Walter when I was leaving the park today. He was on his way to Mr. Forest's office at the top of the tree, appearing very upset about this whole thing."

"Walter?" Gloria made a *tsk* sound. "Well, you play with fire, you're gonna get burned."

"You can't possibly think Walter was involved in the murder!" I gasped.

"No, no," she shook her head, "but spending any time alone with Heather was a poor decision on his part. Baby bunny or no. It's not like she didn't have quite the reputation." She took another sip of her tea, then squeezed some more lemon into it. "Is he up for the operations manager promotion?"

"I doubt it," I said. "But you never know. He looked so frazzled today, it's hard to imagine he's capable of leading *our* department, let alone park operations."

Gloria's eyes glittered. "Why don't you let me come tomorrow and help you poke around?"

I considered that for a moment. Gloria would slow down my pace, but people were comfortable around her. Maybe I could get more out of anyone we questioned if she was there running interference? I planned to return to Ivy's office to get a list of anyone vying for the director of operations position.

"I won't get in your way, I promise." She could tell I was debating her request. "My people have a saying: 'ebry shut eye ain't sleep.'"

"Ah, you're gonna have to translate that one for me." I loved it when she shared her Gullah wisdom with me.

"It means that just because someone doesn't appear to be paying attention doesn't mean they aren't," she said. "I can fly under the radar. But I pick up on things. Important things."

She did have a good eye for details. "Alright. Let's meet there at ten and see who's around to talk to. The press conference is at noon, and I think it's taking place in the park. So we can go to that too."

"I like that idea." She grinned as our server set two steaming-hot plates in front of us.

Tomorrow we would sneak around to gather more clues. Tonight we feasted.

ZOE

I was not a morning cat.

I didn't know too many morning cats, to be honest. Unless it was four o'clock in the morning, and we were ready for breakfast, of course. There was a reason we were known for being nocturnal. *Mornings suck, and we don't get to drink coffee. Enough said.*

But I got up with the sun the following morning because A) I couldn't sleep well knowing my brother had been carried off by that big oaf Jeremy, our handler. He was the one in charge of the cat colony at Fairytale Forest, and he was every bit as dumb as he looked. Maybe dumber.

Oh, and B) I wanted to talk to Cat as soon as I could.

(I'm pretty sure that's the way the bipeds do it: A and then B.)

Ziti was hot on my tail as I started to round the park. "Why are you following me?" I hissed over my shoulder when she got a little too close.

"I care about him too, you know," was all she said.

A shudder rolled through my body as I continued down the main street, passing some custodians emptying the trash, but none of them were Cat. She didn't come in until evening, but with the park closed—and it was still closed, or we'd already have music blaring and smells wafting from the kitchens—she was likely to show up earlier to do some more investigating. I needed to send her a sign, get her attention, without attracting the attention of anyone who meant me harm.

My fear was that Scar and Vinny weren't going to stop at getting Moony hauled off—they would send me packing as soon as the opportunity presented itself. And if I was caught cavorting with Cat—well, that would be opportunity enough for them.

"What are we going to do?" Ziti interrupted my thought process when I got to Storybook Street.

"You can follow me, but you're not allowed to talk."

"Come on, Zoe. I want to help. I want to get Moony back too."

I sighed in resignation. "My plan is to talk to the biped, get her to help us. Maybe she can go to the shelter where they took Moony and get him back before someone adopts him. But I have to figure out how to get her attention first."

Ziti's tail swished back and forth as she cocked her head like a dog and thought. "I've got it!"

This oughtta be good. I didn't think Ziti was especially known for her smarts, but maybe she would surprise me. "Well, give it to me."

"Let's make her a sign," she suggested. "Like a secret message or something."

"A secret message," I repeated. What in the world was she talking about?

She nosed a pinecone that was on the grass over onto the courtyard. "Let's leave her a sign—something so she knows we're looking for her."

"How can we do that? We're cats." Did I really need to remind her of the limitations of our species?

"I think I can use these pinecones." Ziti lifted her paw to point at the one she'd just nosed onto the concrete. "Let's make them into a cat shape."

"Are you for real right now?"

"You have no faith in me whatsoever, do you?" She nosed another pinecone onto the concrete and then whipped around to look at me. "You know, Moony likes me too. And he likes me because I'm smart, and I have good ideas."

"Is that so?"

"Yeah, it is so." She put another pinecone in her mouth and carried it over to the pile she was making. "You know, you *could* help."

"Fine." I helped her move a dozen or so more pinecones into the corner of the walkway. Then she arranged them in a shape she thought looked like a cat, but it really was more like an amoeba in my personal opinion. And, yes, I knew what amoebas were from some documentaries one of the security people enjoyed watching.

I'm telling you, it was very educational watching TV in the security office during my formative years.

She tilted her head toward the bushes. "We should go hide before Scar and Vinny figure out what we're doing."

"Good point." I padded over to the bush and lay down, giving myself a once-over with my tongue. Then I yawned. *Mornings suck.* Hopefully I had time for a nap before Cat arrived.

CATHERINE

Gloria was waiting for me on a bench when I arrived at the park. "Hey, who let you in?" was my first question—she didn't have a magic wand for entry like I did.

"Oh, I know who to talk to." She gave me a wink and stood up, smoothing imaginary wrinkles out of her jungle-print blouse she wore over black leggings.

"I'm sure you do." I had to laugh—Gloria was a whole vibe, and I was here for it. She had about a decade on me, but sometimes she seemed much younger than her age. "So are we watching the press conference first? The detectives are here, and the news people just went in to set up."

"We've still got some time. Let's see if we can talk to someone in security, find out if Rory Blake had any kind of familiarity with our vic."

"With our vic, eh? Those detectives sure have been rubbing off on you!" Gloria smiled as we began our trek down Storybook Street.

She stopped short where the street ended and the courtyard began. "What's that?" She pointed to a cluster of pinecones by the bushes at the edge of the courtyard.

"Pinecones," I retorted. "Looks like they need to be swept up."

"No…I think they're arranged in a pattern of some sort."

We both stepped closer, squinting at the amoeba-like shape the pile had taken on. She was right—something about it didn't quite look random.

She pointed. "Is that a tail?"

"Huh…yeah, it might be."

That was when it hit me. The cats! They were sending a message.

"I think the cats want to have a meeting," I announced— then my hand immediately flew to my mouth, clasping over it with a smack.

"A what now?" I turned around to see that Jayden Forest had joined us.

Oh, great. The cats needed to speak with me, and I had both Gloria and Jayden to contend with. How was I going to accomplish this?

That was when I noticed Zoe stirring in the bushes on the other side of the pinecone pile. She yawned, stretched, then looked right at me. She didn't move her mouth at all, but I heard her say, "Castle?"

I nodded, then whipped around to face my coworkers. I'd have to come up with something snappy if I was going to pull this off. *What to say, what to say? Oh!*

"Hey, Jayden, do you know Rory Blake at all?" I bought myself a little bit of time so I could figure out how to make this work.

Jayden ran his hands through his dark hair, making me realize how much he favored his mother. "Yeah, his son and I played lacrosse together at Porter-Gaud. Why?"

"Well, we need to find out some information about him. Do you think you and Gloria could go and ask him some questions?" I said it more like an order than a request.

"What kind of questions?" Jayden blinked. "Oh, this is about the investigation, isn't it?" His nose scrunched up. "You don't think Rory had something to do with—"

Gloria's eyebrow arch gave it away.

"Wow…okay. So I get to help too?" Excitement sparkled in his dark eyes.

"Why did you come in today?" I asked him. Surely he should be getting the day off along with the other park employees.

He shrugged. "I'm here for the press conference, but I thought I might do a bit of nosing around too. I mean, it's not every day your family's theme park has an employee murdered."

"Well, you can kill two birds with one stone," Gloria quipped before turning toward me. "We can go talk to Rory. But what are *you* gonna be doing, missy?"

"Uh…I need to go check something out over at the

castle. That's where I found the knitting pattern yesterday. I just wanna see if—"

"Fine," Gloria waved her hand dismissively, "let's meet back at the Guest Services building for the press conference at noon."

We had a deal.

Eighteen

ZOE

Ziti and I hid in the shadows while we waited for Cat, who would hopefully be able to ditch her companion to meet us in secret. I had also ditched the rest of my entourage. Well, they were sleeping—so "ditching" might not be quite the correct word. We were cats, so we weren't particularly fussed about choosing the right words. The fact that we used any words at all was bordering miraculous.

I was getting tired of sneaking around and worrying that Scar or Vinny was going to wreak havoc for me or any of my friends. They'd already crossed a line with Moony when I thought we'd agreed to work together to help keep the park open. And now they had gotten my brother expelled from the park and were doing who-knows-what to Priss.

"Zoe?" I heard Cat call from the entrance.

I backed into the corner where we'd had our last chat—knowing it was a spot the cameras couldn't pick up. "In here!" I returned, knowing she would be able to hear me, but no one else would.

"There you are! And Ziti." She nodded at my tabby-striped companion. I was the only one of us who could understand Cat, and she was the only one who could understand me. I wasn't sure what kind of magic was at work here, but as a cat, I wouldn't waste time needlessly worrying about it. Unlike bipeds, we didn't need to know the answer to everything. We were happy with just existing and living our lives. Bipeds could certainly learn a few lessons from us.

"They took my brother," was the first thing out of my mouth when she came into view. "You have to get him back!"

"What? Which one is your brother? Who took him?"

"The handler—Jeremy," I said. "One of the other cat clowders set him up, but that's beside the point. I just need to make sure he's okay and get him back here as soon as possible."

She wrinkled up her face. "I have no idea how to do that."

"You'll have to talk to Jeremy, find out where they took him. Can you please get him back? Please? I'll do anything!" To emphasize my willingness, I rubbed against her legs, weaving in and out between them to show my adorableness and desperation for her attention and help.

"Okay, I'll talk to Jeremy, but I need you to do something for me too," she stated firmly.

"What's that?"

"There are a couple of people I need you to follow, find out if they could be involved in what happened to Heather," she said. "One is Rory Blake, Director of Security—"

"Oh, I know him!" I reflected back fondly on the time

when I was a kitten and Rory was just one of the regular joes in the security office. He was the huge *Law and Order* fan.

"Great!" she exclaimed. "And the other one is Walter McDuff, Director of Facility Services. He's my boss's boss."

"Oh, is that the big doofy-looking guy with the weird orange hair and glasses?"

She exploded with laughter. "Sorry, that was just the most accurate description I've ever heard of him, and it came from a cat."

"Look, lady," I said, my tail twitching back and forth, "we cats are nothing if not observant."

More laughter spilled out. It almost sounded like she was having some sort of fit. I wasn't equipped to administer any medical interventions. "Get it together, Cat. We have work to do, and I need my brother back."

"Alright, I'm headed to talk to Jeremy. Keep me posted. Maybe we can meet back up here later today? Say around four or five o'clock?"

"Well, I don't tell time, Cat, so can you be a little less specific? Or would it be *more* specific?"

She tilted her head in thought. "Meet me back here when four chimes sound off from the clock tower on main street."

"Sounds good."

CATHERINE

On my way to find Jeremy, and possibly Gloria and Jayden, if I just happened to run into them, I remembered the conversation I overheard coming from Heather's office shortly before her body was found.

Heather's voice was low but still southern-fried, "I don't care what you think. I do what I want. You should know that by now. It's a mistake to try to control me because *I'm* the one in control."

There was a short pause and then, "You're gonna regret messing with me. Mark my words."

I wondered if there were any security cameras in the hallway outside Heather's office door, and if I asked Rory Blake nicely enough, would he let me see the footage from that time period? Because she vaguely threatened someone, and that someone could have been her killer.

Then I remembered the niggling feeling I had about Walter. About him not faring well in the wake of Heather's death. I asked Zoe to follow him because I was concerned about his mental health, not because I was worried he offed Heather. I couldn't even imagine him hurting a fly, let alone murdering an actual human being. Heather had screwed him over, yes—she bullied and blackmailed him to cover up Derek Swift's accusation. She walked all over him trying to claw her way into the operations manager position—but he would just sit back and take it, like he had many things throughout the years.

Back to Jeremy the Cat Handler. I honestly wasn't sure what his last name was. Perhaps he was one of those notorious people who only needed one name, like Sting or Slash.

I found the tall, wiry man on the back side of the tree where the entrance to his office was.

The tree's second floor, one level above the security offices, was Jeremy's domain. He had a full kitchen where he made healthy treats for the cats. They weren't fed meals on a regular basis—he just used the treats to lure them when he needed to, to move them around the park or bring them in for medical tests or interventions. And, of course, if he needed to rehome one of the cats.

I used my magic badge to open the door to his lair, calling down the hall first as I didn't want to startle him. "Jeremy? You there? Can I chat with you real quick?"

Something sounding like a grunt traveled back to my ears. I had never spoken to him before, but from what I understood, he was even less effective at communicating than his feline charges.

"Hi, Jeremy," I announced myself as I approached. "I'm Catherine Lyon. I wanted to ask you about one of the cats you took into custody yesterday."

I had gotten a description from Zoe before we parted ways, and I knew her brother's name. I hoped Jeremy would give me the correct info and not some sort of run-around.

He grunted something else but didn't look up from his lunch. His figure was visible through the doorway to the kitchen, perched on a barstool hunched over a bowl of what looked to be stew.

"It was a gray and white long-haired cat named Moony. Do you know anything about him?" I stopped a few feet from him, hoping he heard me.

"Moony," he said. "Yup, took him to the shelter this mornin', as a matter of fact. He was gettin' a little too friendly with the humans. He was seen cavortin' with Walter from Facility Services."

Oh, so he can *speak!* He had a very thick southern drawl.

"Right, Walter. He's my boss. I, uh…I don't really think Moony is too domesticated," I said.

"Why do y'all care?"

"It's just…he belongs here in the park," I argued. "Is there a way to bring him back?"

Jeremy smirked and set his spoon inside what looked to be an empty bowl. "Are ya tryin' to tell me how to do my job?"

"No, not at all." I smiled warmly. I needed information from this guy—ticking him off was not the way to achieve my goal. "Can you at least tell me where you took him?"

He rolled his eyes, mumbled something unintelligible under his breath and handed me a business card for a local cat rescue in Ladson. It was a little out of the way, but I could head up there after the press conference.

I thanked Jeremy for his help—not that he was a fount of information, but I'd take what I could get—and then I headed to the Guest Services building to watch the press conference. On the way, I ran into Gloria and Jayden.

"Well, were you able to see Mr. Blake?" I hoped their mission had been a little more successful than mine.

"Nope, he's not in. He's already gone to the press conference," Jayden answered before Gloria had a chance to.

"But we did find something else interesting," Gloria interjected with a glimmer in her eyes.

"You did? What's that?"

"I found this outside the tree." She reached into the fanny pack she had strapped around her waist and pulled out a folded-up piece of paper—it was an orangey-pink color.

"Is that a salmon-colored form?" My brows quirked.

Jayden laughed. "Yeah, my dad does love his colored forms."

"Well, it is on the same paper as the salmon-colored forms," Gloria said. "But that's not what it is. Here, take a look."

The top said "Volunteer Schedule at Ladson Cat Sanctuary," and underneath was a calendar with times marked on each date, Monday through Friday. And each box also contained a set of initials. I scanned them to see if any of them jumped out at me, but it just looked like a sea of letters.

"Do you think this is relevant to the case?" Jayden scratched at a few scraggly chin hairs he'd apparently missed while shaving.

"I don't know, but this is the same cat sanctuary that's on the business card Jeremy just handed me." I whipped it out of my pocket and waved it in the air.

Gloria and Jayden exchanged looks. "Who in the what now?" Jayden queried, confusion contorting his features.

"Oh, uh…one of the cats got picked up and taken to the sanctuary," I explained, scrambling for a reasonable explanation that didn't involve me talking to the cats. "He's a good cat. Excellent mouser. I think I'm gonna go see if I can adopt him." I puffed out my chest and straightened my spine nice and tall, trying to come off as confident and resolved.

"You're gonna get a cat!" Gloria squealed. "Oh, how wonderful. I love cats. I used to have a whole mess of 'em. I'll have to come visit."

"Why don't you have any now?" Jayden asked.

She brushed away his question. "Doesn't matter now, son. What's important now is we're late for the press conference."

As we walked toward Guest Services together, I was piecing together all the clues in my mind: the 2.75-inch-wide object used to strangle Heather. The knitting needle. The ball of yarn. The baby blanket pattern. Heather's threatening conversation the day before she died.

This volunteer schedule printed on salmon-colored paper probably wasn't related. It could just be a coincidence, of course, that the color matched one of our company's forms—but only the managers had reams of that paper in their offices. That particular form was used for vacation leave. Did one of the managers here volunteer at the cat sanctuary? Maybe I'd find out when I went later.

But for now, it was showtime.

THE PRESS CONFERENCE WAS SET UP IN A SMALL AUDITORIUM at the back of the Guest Services building. It was much smaller than the one where the Forests held the employee meeting just days ago about how they wanted to keep the park open. Obviously, that didn't happen.

No guests meant no money. We were all going to feel the effects of this.

The room had been built to impress investors, with its plush theater seating and enormous screen meant to show videos of happy park guests spending lots and lots of cash. Gloria, Jayden and I slipped into the back row as I observed who had shown up for the meeting: Walter, representing

Facility Services; Ivy, representing Human Resources; and Rory, representing Security. Alongside them were managers of other divisions such as Guest Relations, Ride Operations, Dining Services, and Marketing.

Any of these people could be vying for the Operations Manager position. When I elbowed Gloria and tilted my head toward the row of managers, she nodded knowingly. I loved the fact that we could communicate just fine via gestures. Jayden raised a curious brow, but we didn't need to let him in on our private conversation.

The front of the room was set up with two adjacent eight-feet tables covered in bunting that matched the park's color scheme of magenta, lime-green and orange. The bright colors contrasted with the somber faces of James and Janelle Forest, Detectives Powers and Towers, and the police commissioner.

Perched like snakes, ready to strike, were all the members of the press in front of us. I didn't know all the outfits they represented, but I was sure they included every network news affiliate in Charleston plus all the newspapers. Eight or nine of them, all champing at the bit to sink their teeth into the panel seated in front of them.

The police commissioner opened the conference, discussing the crime in vague terms like "heartbreaking tragedy" and announcing that the "community was healing." You'd never know from his statement that Heather Suka was despised. Though I did feel bad for her son, of course. And any other family or friends she might have had.

Then Mr. Forest made a brief statement, "Thank you all for coming today and helping us shed light on what has been a horrific and devastating blow to our Fairytale Forest family. We are completely blown away by the magnitude of support in the greater Charleston community, and we hope we will be able to open our doors just as soon as the evil person who murdered Heather Suka is arrested. We would love to welcome you into our park and share with you the magic that has delighted visitors for nearly six decades."

The police commissioner said, "Now we'll open the floor for questions. Please raise your hand and wait to be called on." He gestured to a lady wearing a smart charcoal-gray suit in the front row.

First Reporter: "Have you identified any suspects in this case?"

Detective Towers: "We are following up on leads and looking at forensic and other types of evidence, but we aren't able to discuss the particulars of the case at this time."

Second Reporter: "Do you think the killer is a Fairytale Forest employee?"

Mr. Forest: "We could only speculate about that. The crime did happen after hours, but it's possible a guest hid inside the park and attacked Ms. Suka later."

Detective Powers: "We're not ruling anyone out at this point."

That was a lie, I thought smugly. They'd already ruled out several suspects, including myself, and the security cameras at the front didn't show anyone who wasn't an employee leaving the park. To me, that pointed toward an employee.

Third Reporter: "Can you tell us the cause of death?"

Police Commissioner: "We can confirm our medical examiner listed asphyxiation as the cause of death."

Second Reporter: "Does that mean there's no murder weapon? You're not looking for a knife or a gun, for example."

Detective Towers: "We are not at liberty to discuss the murder weapon."

Fourth Reporter: "How long do you believe the park will be closed?"

Mr. Forest: "As long as it takes to arrest a suspect, unfortunately."

Fifth Reporter: "This is the middle of the high season for your park, Mr. Forest. How do you expect this will impact your company and its employees?"

Mr. Forest: "Obviously, there's going to be a terrible impact on the park and employees. Most of our employees are hourly, so if they don't work, they don't get paid. That's just the way our business is set up—most entertainment venues operate that way. We'd like to make the closure for as brief a time as possible, but it's not entirely within our control."

Sixth Reporter: "How can we, as a community, help Fairytale Forest in the interim?"

Mr. Forest: "Thank you for asking. The best thing you can do is, if any of you have any information about the events of that tragic night, or any information pertaining to Heather Suka, please get in touch with Detectives Towers and Powers. We also have set up an anonymous tip line. Then, simply visit the park and support it with your presence and wallets when it reopens. That would help a lot."

They continued to ask questions that made the Forests and the police hedge. This wasn't helping me. I found myself paying more attention to the managers sitting in the row in front of us. Ivy and Rory were passing notes—interesting. I strained, trying to get a look at the piece of paper they were writing on.

I did notice one thing though—it was salmon-colored.

Nineteen

CATHERINE

"Hey, Walter, you feeling better?" I asked him once the press conference was over and everyone started to filter out of the auditorium. Gloria excused herself to use the restroom, and Jayden went to talk to his parents.

"Oh, yeah." He cleared his throat and puffed out his chest. "I wish this case were solved, but..." he shrugged, "what're ya gonna do?"

"Indeed." I smiled, trying to put him at ease. Was there really something to that niggling voice inside that kept telling me he was acting strange and might somehow be involved in Heather's murder?

Walter?

Walter who once called someone from security to remove a large spider from his office?

I tried to envision him using his hands on someone—

nope, just couldn't see it. Could he strangle a woman with a belt of some sort?

No, it was insanity. I just didn't believe he had it in him. Not even in the heat of the moment—a crime of passion. Whoever did this knew…they knew what they were doing. It was premeditated. They turned off the cameras!

We had to look into Rory Blake more closely. I should have had Zoe concentrate on him, not Walter.

"What about you?" he finally said. "Are you okay?"

"Yeah, of course. Why wouldn't I be?"

"Well, you discovered her body," he reminded me.

"Yeah… That was definitely not my best night at work." I didn't mean it to be funny, but I snickered a little bit at the absurdity of it.

"What are you doing here, Cat?" he questioned.

"You didn't hear? The Forests and the police both asked me to help with the investigation. You know, feel some people out. I have insights about this place they don't."

His eyes narrowed ever so briefly. "You sure do. You're a good choice to help them out." He smiled and rubbed his hands together. "Well, I better get back to my office. I need to finish things up and get home. My wife has a thing tonight, so I need to start dinner. We're having jambalaya!"

"Yum!" Gloria heard him on her way back from the bathroom. "Guess we know where to go for dinner tonight —Walter's house!"

He gave an uneasy laugh. "I'd be totally fine with that if Carol wasn't so funny about having people over when the house isn't in tip-top shape."

"Oh, I'm just giving you a hard time," Gloria insisted, patting his arm. "You get on home to that wife of yours. I'm sure she'll be so glad to come home from her meeting to a nice dinner of jambalaya."

He gave another stiff smile. "Thanks, ladies. See you soon."

Gloria shook her head as he walked away. "Don't even think it, Cat. There's no way he put his hands on that woman, even if she was screwing him over."

I sighed, still trying to soothe the niggling feeling I had. "You don't think he's going out for the operations manager position, do you?"

"Walter? No, he's the least competitive person I know. At the company Christmas party, he wouldn't even play poker. Heck, he wouldn't even play Monopoly!" She chuckled as we headed back outside.

"I'm gonna look for that cat at the shelter," I told Gloria.

"That's a pretty reckless thing to do. What are you gonna do with a cat, Cat?" Gloria smirked.

"I'm hoping to bring him right back here," I said honestly. "I'm going to slip him back in with the other cats."

"Yeah, well, good luck with that. Fairly certain Jeremy will notice if there's an extra cat prowling about—especially one he just personally removed a few days ago."

"If worse comes to worse, I'll keep him for myself," I decided. Zoe could come too, if she wanted. Maybe it was time I had some companions. Maybe I was hearing Zoe talk because I needed a cat in my life?

There had to be some sort of reasonable explanation for it, but right now it was benefiting me since she was helping me solve this murder. I liked to think our partnership was mutually beneficial.

I waved goodbye to Gloria as she headed for the park

exit, and lo and behold, I'd conjured up the feline in question.

ZOE

I staked out Cat and waited for her friend to leave before getting her attention with a high-pitched trill. Her head immediately whipped toward my position behind the dumpster on the side of the building.

She gestured around the back of the building and then headed in that direction. I followed. I couldn't wait to share what I learned with her.

"So I've been following that male," I relayed, and she nodded. "He was talking on his phone."

Her eyes widened. "Go on."

"Right before you all went inside for that meeting."

Her head tilted to the side. "Right...what did he say?"

"I could only hear his words, not whoever he was talking to, but..."

I was a cat, so I did have a decent memory, though maybe not biped-level. I remembered things relatively easily, but whether or not I chose to act on the knowledge gained from those memories was a different topic altogether. Let's just say a faulty memory was not why cats needed nine lives. We needed them due to ignoring said memory.

"Spill the tea, girl!" Cat begged.

"Spill what now?" My whiskers twitched in annoyance. I would tell this story at my own pace, thank you very much.

"Can you please just tell me what you heard Walter say on the phone?" her tone had turned from begging to sugary-sweet.

"Something like, 'I know you volunteer tonight. Yes, I'll start dinner. No, they didn't say anything new at the press conference.'"

"Okay, so he was talking to his wife," Cat said. "I just spoke with him. That all checks out, Zoe. I don't think there's anything unusual there."

"Fine. Well, I tried." I started to walk away.

"Wait," she called me back. "Look, keep on him, okay? And Rory Blake. Keep watching them. I'll be back later, hopefully."

"With Moony?" I asked with a purr of hope.

"Fingers crossed."

"I don't have fingers, Cat."

"Paws crossed?" she tried again. "Claws? Toe beans?"

I shook my head and sauntered away.

CATHERINE

I parked in the gravel lot at the Ladson Cat Sanctuary. It wasn't much to look at—a small one-story building with faded blue siding that appeared to have been built in the sixties or seventies. The windows were encased in black trim, and a welcome mat with paws sat the front door, which was also painted black. The sign by the doorbell said, "Don't ring the bell. Just come in."

I could follow directions, so I twisted the door handle and pushed. The stiff door swung open after I gave it a bit of a shove, and then I had to exert the same effort to close it. A blue faux-granite counter with a smiling receptionist behind it greeted me. On the walls, painted a shade of light grayish-blue, were black-and-white photographs of cats of all breeds, shapes and sizes.

The receptionist's dark hair was piled on her head in a messy bun, and she wore big glasses with tortoiseshell frames. "How may we help you?"

I looked around, not sure who the "we" referred to. "Uh, hi. I'm looking for a cat."

"Oh!" Her expressive hazel eyes widened. "We have lots of cats! Are you looking for a kitten? A calico? A tabby? We just got a litter of super cute—"

"I'm looking for a particular cat that was brought in yesterday," I explained. "His name is Moony, and he's got long gray fur with a few white patches."

"Oh." She scrunched up her nose.

"Is there a problem? I was told he's here."

"Is he your cat, ma'am?"

I could just tell by her expression it wouldn't be wise to tell the truth. I wasn't much for lying, but I didn't have time to deal with a lot of red tape. I just wanted to get Moony and get back to the park.

"Of course he's my cat!" I feigned a little exasperation for effect.

"Oh, okay. Well, let me see here…" She lowered her gaze to the monitor on her desk and began typing furiously on her keyboard.

Now I had to hope and pray Moony came to me like he knew me. He did know me. But he was a cat; therefore, cooperation was not to be expected.

"Oh, he's in 26," she said, looking up at me with a smile. "We just love reuniting pets with their owners."

"Can I see him?"

"Uh, sure. Did you bring a carrier?"

"Oh, um—"

I could see how this looked. I wasn't prepared to take home a cat I was told was here and I had declared belonged to me.

"His carrier was lost in a fire," I lied. "I'm really sorry. Do you have one I can borrow?"

"Oh." She frowned. "I'm sorry to hear that." She stood up, smoothing her olive-green shirt. "Follow me."

She directed me behind the counter and through a large steel door that led to the back of the building. When she unlocked the cat room, I heard a meow or two, but they weren't very loud. The numbered cages started in the left-hand corner and made a U-shape around the room. Twenty-six was in the middle, and sure enough, there was Moony.

Then a woman turned toward me. "Cat! Well, Catherine Lyon, how the heck are you?"

"Oh, hi, Carol!" It was Carol, Walter's wife. *Oh, I guess this is where she volunteers.* I remembered the phone call Zoe reported to me right before I left the park.

She immediately closed the distance between us and wrapped her arms around me. I caught a faint whiff of coconut and flowers. "I haven't seen you since the Christmas party, Cat."

I smiled, taking in her sharp features and curly blonde

hair. "No, that's what happens when Walter and I are on opposite shifts. I really appreciate the treats you bake for us though."

The receptionist just stood to the side, watching our interchange unfold without saying a word. Then, when there was an awkward silence, she chirped, "She's here for the longhair gray and white guy in 26."

"Oh, that's Moony!" Carol gushed. Then her smile faded, and a frown took its place. "But Jeremy just brought him in yesterday. Said he'd gotten too friendly with the park employees…particularly Walter. My husband's always had a way with cats."

I had to think quick. "Yes, but Jeremy said I could have him, so I came to pick him up."

The receptionist—she'd never given me her name— looked displeased. "You said he was already yours."

"Well, he is," I scrambled, "in that he was promised to me. I already know him. See?"

I walked over to Moony and stuck my finger in one of the holes of his cage. He sniffed it carefully. Then he rubbed up against it.

"See?"

Thank you, Moony, for cooperating. He must really be anxious to get out of here.

"Yes, okay," the receptionist finally said, but she still sounded unsure. She glanced over to Carol as if to ask for her opinion.

"Cat is a wonderful human," Carol praised. "I'm sure Moony will be very happy with her."

"Alrighty then, I'll get the paperwork." The receptionist sighed as if daunted by doing her job.

"I didn't know you volunteer here," I said to Carol after the receptionist scurried out the door.

"Oh, yes. I have for several years. I helped connect Jeremy with this shelter to take the socialized and retired cats from Fairytale Forest. And when a litter of kittens gets dumped here, they have a special place to hold them until they're ready to introduce to the colony in the park."

"Wow, that's great. Thanks for helping out. I know the cats make my job easier." I grinned and stroked Moony's fur through the cage.

"Sugar, it's my pleasure." She went over to the corner and sat in a rocking chair. Bending down, she pulled a sweetgrass basket, the kind Gullah women like Gloria still made by hand, off a low shelf of the adjacent bookcase. Then she took a small, half-knitted blanket out of a canvas tote bag. "I lost my yarn," she explained, "so I started the next section in blue."

The portion of blanket knitted in red yarn was about three inches wide.

Twenty

CATHERINE

I had Moony in the carrier and made it as far as my car before panic began to set in. It was all making sense to me now.

Walter's wife was the killer.

And she had used the unfinished blanket she was knitting for the shelter cats to strangle Heather. She must have dropped her knitting needle, ball of yarn, and the volunteer schedule Walter had printed out for her on salmon-colored paper on his office printer when she scrambled to get out of the park.

So why didn't security have her leaving the park? She must have gotten out another way.

Then I realized she had delivered cookies to Walter's office the next morning, which meant—she didn't leave. He must have hidden her in his office. And he must have been the one to turn off the cameras as well.

If I was going to prove this, I needed that blanket. I didn't want to leave the shelter without it.

"Moony, I don't know if you can understand me, but I need your help."

He lifted a paw and stared at me, his intense green eyes glowing in the late afternoon sun. I couldn't hear anything from him like I could Zoe, but he seemed to understand me.

"We're going to go back inside, and I'm going to set your carrier down, unlocked. I want you to go get the blanket Carol was knitting while I create a distraction. I'll pretend I left my phone in there and get them to help me search for it. Okay?"

He blinked a few times and lowered his chin as if to show he was ready.

"Thanks. I'll get you back to the park as soon as I can, okay?"

I grabbed the carrier and unlocked the front, closing the door but leaving it unlatched. Then I took a deep breath and headed back inside the shelter. This had to work. I had to get my hands on that blanket, but I couldn't let Carol know I was on to her.

"Oh, coming back so soon?" Carol greeted me on her way out the door. She had a canvas tote bag with a pithy quote about knitting slung over her shoulder. The corner of the blanket she'd been working on poked out of the top.

Drat! She was getting away with the evidence.

"Oh, yeah, I think I may have left my phone inside," I explained then glanced down at the carrier. Moony looked up at me with wide, questioning eyes. "Aren't you leaving a little early? I thought Walter said you would be home for a late dinner."

She sighed. "He just called me. He wants me to come to his office, something about the detectives asking him for proof of his alibi during the murder." She *tsked* and shook her head. "As if Walter could ever be involved in something so heinous. He was home in bed—with me." She rolled her eyes, then her expression morphed into one of sadness. "It's terrible what happened to her though. You worked with Heather too, didn't you?"

"I did," was all I said. "Well, I don't want to keep you from helping the police."

She smiled. "Thanks. Have a good night. I'll tell Walter you picked a great cat!"

"Thanks, Carol." I gave a little awkward wave, then headed inside the building so she wouldn't be suspicious. I watched her climb into her car and drive off into the sunset. I had no time to lose.

"We're closing soon," the receptionist said from the desk. "Did you need something else?"

"Oh, I thought I lost my phone, but I found it." I patted my pocket, gave her a lopsided smile and hightailed it back to my car. I was returning to the park immediately.

THE FIRST THING I DID WAS CALL GLORIA. I TOLD HER WHAT happened and asked her to meet me at the park.

I spoke to Moony on the drive, and though he wasn't answering me, I'd like to think he was absorbing every word and providing moral support. "I just don't understand what drove her to do it, though. I mean, she may have heard the rumors about Walter and Heather, but didn't she believe her husband?"

After pulling into the entrance for the park, I took the long loop around to the employee parking lot. I was grateful the Forests had given me this all-access badge, or else how would I sneak in like I planned to do with this cat?

"And another thing—I called Walter right after it happened, and he was in bed, just like Carol said. I thought he'd said something to her. Wasn't she in bed next to him?"

Then it hit me. The night we found Heather's body, my nerves were an absolute frazzled mess. The first thing I did was call Walter's cell phone. He could have answered my call from anywhere—even from inside the park. He was probably holed up in his office with her. Maybe he pretended to be awakened abruptly, just an act to cover up his wife's crime.

That red flash I saw when I discovered the body—that wasn't the attacker fleeing because no non-employees were caught on camera leaving the park. But it very well could have been Carol with the murder weapon trailing behind her like a scarf. Maybe she went to the exit and realized she'd be caught if she left, so she looped back around to the custodial building, where her husband's office was.

But did she plan to murder Heather? Was that why he had the cameras turned off? How did she get Heather to meet with her? Why did it happen on the main street of the park?

I still had so many questions.

I put my Rogue in park and tried to formulate a plan. I'd told Gloria to meet me outside Guest Services, but I wanted to reunite Moony with Zoe and give them some instructions so they could help me.

"I can't just carry you into the park in this carrier," I said to him. "I have to be stealth about this. Sneak you in."

I looked in my back seat and spotted a shopping bag I used to carry home groceries. "That'll work. You're gonna have to be extra quiet and still, okay?"

Resignation appeared on his face when I lifted him out of the carrier and ushered him into the bag. *Cats love bags, right? Shouldn't be a problem.* "Stay out of sight," I reminded him as I clicked my key fob to lock my doors.

Gloria pulled in next to me and was out of her car a lot faster than I expected a woman of her age to move. Her usual colorful scarf had been replaced by a soft pink silk bonnet. "I was just settling in for the night, so this is how y'all are getting me." She gestured to her short-sleeved pink floral housecoat and matching pink flip-flops.

"You look perfect!" I declared as the bag slung over my shoulder began to move.

"Do I even want to know?" Gloria eyed the bag.

"Prob'ly not. C'mon, we don't wanna miss our chance." I gestured for her to lead the way.

But she wasn't moving. At least not yet. "Now tell me again why you think sweet Carol McDuff could possibly be behind this?"

I explained everything I'd laid out to Moony on the drive over as we headed inside the park. My badge got us all in perfectly. Then I realized there was a slight snag in my plan.

I was going to have Moony run to get Zoe, and then I was going to tell them both how I needed their help to distract everyone in the conference room. But Gloria was with me. She would see me talking to the cats—something I had been trying to avoid.

I huffed out a breath. Well, I'd come this far.

Wait, I could send her in ahead of me, then tell Moony to go find his sister. *Yeah, duh. Of course.*

When we reached Guest Services, I turned to Gloria. "You go on inside. I've gotta return Moony here to where he belongs outside the view of the cameras, then I'll be right in."

Gloria just stood there, staring at me with a funny expression on her face. Then she cocked her hip out and put one fist on it.

"What?"

She stood there for a moment, just blinking.

"Go on," I urged her. I didn't have time for her dramatics.

"If you think I don't know you've been talking to those cats, you are dumber than I thought, Catherine Lyon."

My heart rate spiked. "What?"

"Just do what you need to do. It will look less suspicious if we go in together. You're gonna be helping me look for my phone. I may have dropped it somewhere in the building during the press conference." She gave me an overly animated wink.

Ah, the old lost phone trick.

"Okay, fine, you're right." I sighed. "You don't think I'm a freak?"

She reached out and patted my arm. "If you're a freak, you're the very best kind. Now do what you need to do."

I nodded and led her around the corner to where there weren't any cameras. "Go find Zoe and get back here as soon as you can."

He raced off with absolutely no hesitation. Minutes later, he was back, his pink tongue hanging out of his panting mouth as Zoe practically ran right into my shins but stopped herself at the last moment.

"Thank you, thank you, thank you!" she cried, her eyes darting between me and her brother, who was still recovering from his Paul Revere-esque run.

I gave them instructions, Zoe nodded, and they were on their way. They were going to use their rivalry with the mafia cats—as she called them—to our advantage.

I only had one more issue to solve, and we could get inside and alert the police we'd identified the suspect. The cats would need access to the building.

Mr. and Mrs. Forest were heading toward the Guest Services building.

"Why, good evening, Ms. Lyon," Mr. Forest greeted me, tipping his hat like we'd time-traveled to the nineteenth century. "Are you still working on the case? The detectives just called me and said they got a confession."

"A confession?" I blinked. Were we not needed?

"Yes, Walter McDuff has confessed to Heather Suka's murder," Mrs. Forest said, obvious disdain dripping off his words.

"No, no. That's not right." I shook my head. "No—I have to stop him—"

"What do you mean?" Mr. Forest's brow arched, and he gave his wife a concerned look.

"Sir, I need your help. In a few minutes, there are going to be a couple of cats running this way. It may seem completely crazy, but, please, just trust me—the integrity of this whole case rests on this moment. Can y'all just open the door for them?"

"What? I—what are you talking about?" he stammered.

Gloria stood up tall in her pink housecoat and bonnet.

"Sir, Cat would never ask y'all to do anything if it wasn't completely necessary. Please trust her. She's got this."

Mrs. Forest shrugged and jerked on her husband's sleeve. "Let's just do what she says, James."

They both nodded, and we rushed inside, headed for the elevator and made our way up to the conference room with our hearts pounding a mile a minute.

It all came down to this.

Twenty-One

ZOE

I'd been ruminating all day about what to do re: Scar, Vinny, and Princess. The fact that they were holding her hostage was not working for me. It was very much the antithesis of my personal philosophy on how things should operate in our cat colony. You can imagine that getting my brother expelled from the park was equally infuriating. Carefully harnessing that anger and intense need for revenge, I was able to formulate an operation that would restore order to our little feline world.

I rubbed my paws together in anticipation. I couldn't wait to see if it worked.

"Okay, so you're clear on the plan?" I voiced to my crew as they surrounded me like sports bipeds gathered around a coach during a…timeout…*I think they're called.*

I gazed across the faces of my loyal soldiers: Moony, Ice, Cool, Ziti, Amber, Sass, Daisy and… "Hank, wake up, buddy. We need you. It's all hands on deck."

Hank's bleary eyes blinked open. "What did I miss?"

"Just wake up and follow us," Ziti commanded, and I shot her a dirty look since I was the only one who should be giving out orders.

This was a motley crew, but they were mine.

And we were going to do this. I puffed out my chest and addressed my feline army: "First, we find Vinny and Scar."

I'd been waiting a long time to do this, and vengeance was soon to be mine.

CATHERINE

We stepped off the elevator and immediately heard an anguished confession coming from the conference room. "I did it! I killed Heather Suka," Walter's deep voice wailed.

I rushed into the room. "No, wait, don't listen to him!" I blurted out, my heart racing and lungs heaving.

The police commissioner—*whoops, didn't expect to see him here*—stood up. "Ms. Lyon, I presume? I don't believe your services are required any longer. Mr. McDuff is confessing to the crime."

"But he didn't do it!" I insisted. "If you can just give me a moment, I can prove he didn't do it and who actually did!" I patted the bag that still rested on my shoulder. It was now empty of cats, but there were other important items in it: the rosewood knitting needle, a sample of the red yarn, the baby blanket knitting pattern, and the volunteer schedule for the Ladson Cat Shelter printed on salmon-colored paper.

Just then, Carol McDuff stood up and addressed the commissioner, as well as Detectives Powers and Towers, who were seated next to him. "Sirs, ma'am, I don't think it's right that Catherine is allowed to be here. I know she helped you with the investigation, but my husband deserves his privacy and dignity. Ms. Lyon is one of his subordinates," she seethed, her short blonde curls shaking with each word she carefully enunciated.

Gone was her sweet voice and demeanor. Standing before me was a woman who was going to let her husband fall on his sword for her. And I was not about to have it.

"They caught me tampering with the video equipment," Walter told me, his eyes filled with pain and regret. "I just wanted that promotion so bad. I couldn't let Heather stand in my way—and she was blackmailing me. I just wanted the problem to—"

Before he could say another word, there was a thunderous crash outside the room, followed by a cacophony of hisses, screeches, and ear-piercing shrieks, which filled the air as a massive tangle of paws, tails, and teeth tumbled into the room.

Mr. and Mrs. Forest stood in the doorway, their eyes wide. Mrs. Forest clutched her chest and looked to her husband to stop this madness. But no human in their right mind would get in the middle of that craziness!

The cat brawl continued, knocking over chairs and furniture, rattling the windowpanes, and sending everyone flying. Papers and cups of coffee on the table were overturned, and the air hung heavy with the smell of angry cat musk. Out of the corner of my eye, I saw Zoe waiting for her moment to strike.

"I'm calling Jeremy," Mr. Forest said, whipping out his phone.

And then, just like that, the battle traveled out the conference room door, down the hallway and, if my hearing was accurate, down the staircase.

"Wow, what was all that about?" Carol shook her head as she went to the sink in the corner of the room to retrieve napkins. Gloria and I sprang into action to help her clean up the overturned coffees. While we were crouched down at one end of the table, she snarled in my ear, "You won't get away with this."

I laughed because I could see I already had. The cats had performed expertly, and I was about to lay out my case.

"Walter, please don't throw yourself under the bus for your wife," I said. And then I asked an all-important question: "Are you a knitter?"

"What?" His brows furrowed. "No, of course not. Carol is, though."

"Exactly." I pulled the clues out of the shopping bag and presented them to the detectives. "This knitting needle belongs to Carol. And I have a feeling you'll find its mate with Carol's belongings. It's a rare, expensive rosewood needle, not a common one you'd see just anywhere. Oh, and remember that red yarn we found tangled in the bushes in the Haunted Wood? I think you'll find it matches the yarn used in the murder weapon."

"Murder weapon?" Detective Towers gasped. "What do you mean?"

"Mrs. McDuff knits blankets for the cats at the Ladson Cat

Sanctuary, where she volunteers. She was there this afternoon knitting a blanket where the first three inches are red, and the rest is blue. She confessed that she lost her ball of red yarn—"

"She's crazy!" Carol screamed, leaping to her feet. She clutched her large canvas tote in her hand and quickly threw it over her shoulder. "I'm not going to stay here and listen to this outrageous crock of—"

I took a deep breath and raised my volume, effectively talking over her. "I think you'll find that the blanket Carol is currently working on was used to strangle Heather Suka," I continued, my eyes laser-focused on the detectives and commissioner and not giving one iota of attention to Carol, who was turning nearly purple with rage.

"That's completely false! She's making all of that up!" she seethed, gripping the canvas bag tight to her chest. "You're going to believe this stupid janitor when my husband has devoted two decades of service to this park?"

Just then, Zoe stepped out from under the table with a half-finished blanket in her mouth. One end was made from red yarn, and the rest was blue.

"Oh, you mean this one? The one with the matching rosewood knitting needle stuck in it?" I pointed to the end of the blanket where she'd hastily stopped stitching earlier today. Then I looked closer. "Oh—and there's a reddish-blonde hair tangled in it that looks waaaaay longer than the ones on your head. How much do you want to bet it's a match to Heather?"

"You can't prove that belongs to me!" she shrieked.

"I can," Gloria announced, standing up. She pulled her cell phone out of her pocket and smiled. "I snapped this picture of it poking out of that same bag that's on your shoulder now as soon as I came into the room—just before our friend Zoe here nabbed the evidence."

Zoe proudly carried the half-finished blanket over to the detectives and dropped it at their feet.

"Thank you, Zoe," I said as Gloria passed around her phone with the image of the blanket in Carol's knitting bag.

"It's not even my bag!" Carol lied. "I just brought it home from the shelter on accident. I meant to grab—"

"Honey, it has your name on it," Walter said, shaking his head. "Sit down. It's time to come clean about what really happened."

Carol gave a defeated sigh as she yanked a chair back from the table and plopped down in it. "I wanted Walter to get the promotion," she confessed. "He works so hard, and he never speaks up for himself. He deserves it. He's been here a long time, and he's always done a great job. I wasn't going to let someone like Heather stand in his way. And then she tried to blackmail him—"

Walter put his arm around his wife and turned toward the detectives. "Carol asked me to set up a meeting between her and Heather. She wanted to have a woman-to-woman discussion with her and ask her to drop out of consideration for the operations manager job."

"Go on," Detective Towers said as she and her partner scribbled down some notes.

"Well, when I asked Heather to meet her, she was nasty about it," Walter relayed. "She agreed to do it, but she said something about how it was a mistake to try to control her because she was the one in control."

I gasped. "It was you I overheard Heather talking to before the TP meeting!"

He nodded sadly. "They were meeting in the bakery

right at park closing, and I…well, I just wanted it off the record, so I asked Rory to turn off the cameras in that section of Storybook Street. Rory didn't know why I asked, I swear. He didn't even really question me."

"Probably because you've only ever helped people," Gloria spoke up. "You don't have a mean bone in your body, Walter. We all know that. We all knew you weren't capable of murder. And you probably don't want that promotion either, do you?"

He shook his head and looked down at his hands, which were now laced tightly together in his lap. "No, but Carol wanted me to have it. I wanted her to be proud of me. I wanted her to—"

"You deserved that promotion," Carol insisted. "You still do." Then she turned to the detectives. "Heather met me at the bakery at the appointed time, and we had coffee together. I told her to back off Walter and drop out of the race. I knew she wasn't going to back down easily, but I wasn't expecting what she did do."

"Which was what?" Detective Powers asked.

Carol's nostrils flared as she considered her words carefully. Her chest heaving and fire in her eyes, she finally spoke. "We were leaving the bakery, still arguing about Walter. When we made it out onto the sidewalk, she told me something disgusting about my husband. Something she had supposedly done with him, and I—" she visibly shuddered, "—well, I just completely lost it at that point."

She sucked in a breath, her face streaked with tears as the confession gurgled up her throat. "I reached into my bag and pulled out the blanket I had started knitting for the shelter. It was about the size of a thin scarf. And I flung it around her neck, crossed the ends and tugged it tight. I told her to take back what she said about Walter and admit she was lying—"

I looked over at Walter as a tear slipped down his cheek. This was hard for him to hear.

"She wouldn't take it back!" Carol seethed. "She wouldn't take it back!" She burst into tears, a string of unintelligible words streaming out as Detective Powers stood up and went around to the back of her chair, taking her by the arm, and forcing her to her feet.

Within moments, she was handcuffed and being escorted out of the building while Walter sat with his face buried in his hands.

Twenty-Two

ZOE

We gathered around under the bushes as the activity in the park dwindled. It was near closing time, and fireworks burst in the sky over the tree, and the smell of popcorn still wafted on the air. Sound of bipeds cheering, "Oooh! Ahhhh!" underscored the music soundtrack blaring from park speakers as the farewell show played out.

I looked around the faces of my clowder in a semi-circle around me: Moony, Mr. Cool Cat, Hank, Ice, Daisy, Ziti, Amber, Sass and…our new addition…Princess. Ziti was cozied up with Moony as Ice inched closer and closer to Princess. Love was in the air.

"Thank you so much for rescuing me," Princess said, her voice wobbly with emotion—well, as much emotion as a cat can muster. "I was miserable over there with the mafia cats." A shudder racked her chocolate fur as she thought about it.

"I'm glad it worked out. No cat deserves that kind of

treatment," I assured her. "And it just so happened that rescuing you was the perfect trigger to get Scar, Vinny and his thugs to chase us into the Guest Services building."

"I'm just glad we were able to help get the park back open," Cool said. "I'm too old to start over as someone's pet."

"We're lucky Cat was able to communicate with us." I sighed. "All's well that ends well, I suppose."

"I heard Vinny and Scar are terrorizing another clowder," Ice shared. "I hate to get involved, but—"

"I really thought maybe we could work together for once." I stretched my paws, watching my claws appear and disappear as I flexed them. "If he wants to act like a scumbag, he will be treated accordingly. I'm not going to let him mess up the good life we enjoy at the park."

"Hear, hear!" Amber agreed.

Hank sighed. "Thanks, Zoe, for taking care of us."

"Thank you, Zoe," a chorus around me echoed.

I puffed out my chest. It was nice to be appreciated.

For once.

CATHERINE

"Really, Mr. Forest, none of this is necessary." I scanned the room, my eyes bugging out at the tables full of food and, in the center, a giant cake with the words "Thank you, Cat!" written in scrolling magenta frosting.

"Please, call me James." He extended his hand for me to

shake as his wife held out a glass of champagne. I thought it was for her husband, but she handed it to me instead.

"Thanks to you," Mrs. Forest said, "the park was only closed for a few days, and Heather Suka's murderer is behind bars."

"I'm happy to be of service," I said before sipping the champagne. "But I had help. Gloria, of course, and even your son, Jayden, helped me figure it out."

"We're just so happy to have you on our team. Hopefully we'll never have to deal with anything like that happening at the parks ever again!" Mr. Forest sighed as he raised his glass. "Join me in a toast, everyone."

Gloria grabbed a tall flute of sparkling champagne off a passing waiter's tray and came to stand next to me. She looked elegant in a black tunic with gold sequins and shiny black cropped pants. Her hair—usually covered by a scarf or wrap—was a crown of beautifully intricate braids all twisted into an elegant bun on the top of her head.

"Ladies, gentlemen, our Fairytale Forest family, and distinguished guests," Mr. Forest began his toast. "Thank you all for coming together this evening to celebrate one of our own. Ms. Catherine Lyon is such an asset to this organization. Not only has she provided decades of loyal service in the facilities services department, but during recent events, she went above and beyond to investigate the crime that occurred on our premises. She aided the police investigation and was able to crack the case due to her diligence and keen perception. We are grateful for everything she and her coworker, Gloria Bress, have done for Fairytale Forest, and to thank them, we are pleased to offer them each an honorarium in the amount of ten thousand dollars."

My jaw nearly dropped to the floor. *Ten thousand dollars? Whew!*

Gloria looked like her face might split in two, she was smiling so broadly. Mr. Forest offered me the microphone, but I declined. I wasn't much of a public speaker, and I had no desire to be a public figure of any kind.

I just wanted to enjoy my job and my simple life here in the lowcountry. It was nice to have a little excitement, but I'd had enough now to last me for a while. Perhaps I'd take my windfall and go pay my sons a visit. Maybe a little maternal meddling might spur them a little closer to making me a grandmother…

"You aren't going home?" Gloria asked as we exited the auditorium at the back of the Haunted Woods and headed toward the front of the park.

"I am eventually, but I think I want to just walk for a few minutes—you know, enjoy this fine evening," I answered.

"Mmmhmmm. You wanna talk to your cats. Don't think you can pull one over on me, friend." Gloria grinned, and the moonlight painted silver strokes across her features.

"Okay, you got me," I confessed. "But I'll see you tomorrow night for work?"

"Yes, ma'am, you will. Now I'm gonna go home and dream about what to do with all this cash." She waved her check in the air. "But I feel like you deserve this more than me. You did most of the work."

"Nonsense," I maintained. "You deserve it just as much as

I do. Use it for something selfish, something you'll really enjoy."

"Oh, I will. Have no doubt about that!" She gave me a hug and wandered down the path toward the tree.

I came to the bushes where the cats normally congregated. "Zoe, you there?" I whispered, not sure if anyone was within earshot.

The beautiful gray longhaired cat sauntered out from the bushes. "You rang?" She sat, her bushy tail curled around her as she looked up into my eyes.

"I just wanted to thank you again," I said, "for everything."

"No, thank you," Zoe insisted. "Not sure what we would have done if you hadn't been around the night we found the body."

"It worked out well," I agreed. "I still can't believe I can understand you. That you can understand me."

"We can understand most bipeds," she reminded me. "We just don't always choose to listen."

"Right."

Silence hung between us as crickets chirped from the bushes and frogs croaked from the banks of the river just yards away. "Well...guess I better get on home."

"I better go catch some mice." Her lips turned up ever so slightly, the closest thing to a smile I'd ever seen on a cat.

"Don't be a stranger..." I called after her as she slunk back into the bushes.

I heard her faint voice respond, "Don't be too friendly..."

Epilogue

A h, yes, the vile dragoness is slain, and that annoying manager's wife is behind bars. It pays to have enemies. At least it pays me.

The mastermind behind the murder chuckled as their eyes caught on the newspaper article. "The park was only closed for a few days? That will never do."

Their fists clenched as they vowed, "I won't rest until Fairytale Forest is closed FOREVER!"

THE END

Follow Cat, Zoe, and the gang on their next adventure here: Felines of Fairytale Forest

Join my newsletter for updates, giveaways and more! Bit.ly/KLMontgomerynews

Acknowledgments

So many wonderful people and other mammals helped me with this book, it's hard to know where to start. First, thank you to my wonderful travel companions who spent time in the Charleston area with me the week I began writing this book.

Rebecca and Yvonne, I had so much fun touring the plantation, looking for shark's teeth, enjoying a fancy meal at 82 Queen, laughing about weird clown/flower paintings, and learning about the ghosts of Charleston on our carriage tour. I laughed so hard, had too much to drink, and came away with not only memories to last a lifetime, but also plenty of material and ideas for this series. Even though I'd visited Charleston so many times, it helped seal the deal that this was the perfect setting for Fairytale Forest.

Also, a HUGE shoutout to Rebecca for letting me crash at her place in North Carolina for a writing retreat while I waited for my next book signing. It was the perfect mix of relaxation and structure, and I am grateful for your wonderful southern hospitality. Not to mention, your lovely cat was a great source of inspiration with all her antics.

Huge thank you to my son, Kadan, for taking my vision for Fairytale Forest and bringing it to life in the map at the front of the book. Your attention to detail and creative flair are very much appreciated, and I know readers will love having a visual reference for the theme park in the series.

Thank you to my amazing friend and proofreader, Tina. I love how I tell you for weeks and months that I'm sending you a book, and you patiently wait, and then when I finally drop it in an email with little or no warning, you rearrange your whole life to get it done quickly. I'm trying to get my act together, I promise! But after sixty books, it's not terribly likely.

Thank you to my friend and promoter, Colleen Noyes of Itsy Bitsy Book Bits. I haven't written an acknowledgment for a while, but any one I write is sure to include you, owing to the fact that you are awesome at what you do and an all-around amazing human being.

Thank you to my own two cats, Zelda and Zulu, who allowed me to observe them as well as give them plenty of scritches and treats. Thank you for giving me odd looks and confirming that you weren't actually going to respond when I tried talking to you.

And, as always, thank you to my family who puts up with my weird writerly ways. And to my two doggos, Indy and Hawking, who are jealous I chose to write about cats.

About the Author

K.L. Montgomery writes bodypositive sweet romance, romcom, and cozy mystery. A librarian in a former life, she now works as an editor and runs the 6000-member Indie Author Support group on Facebook in addition to publishing under two names.

Though she remains a Hoosier at heart, K.L. shares her coastal Delaware home with some furry creatures and her husband, who is on the furry side as well. She has an undying love for her three sons, Broadway musicals, the beach, Seinfeld, the color teal, IU basketball, paisleys, and dark chocolate.

facebook.com/greencastles

instagram.com/k.l.montgomery

bookbub.com/authors/k-l-montgomery

tiktok.com/@klmontgomeryauthor

amazon.com/stores/K.L.-Montgomery/author/B00V2IEEUQ

Also by K.L. Montgomery

Felines of Fairytale Forest

Murder by Moonlight

MORE COMING SOON

Dangerous Curves Series

Betrayal at the Beach

Mystery at the Marina

Shooting at the Shore

Poisoned at the Pier

Bribery on the Boardwalk

Homicide at High Tide

Mischief Under the Mistletoe

Panic at the Playhouse

Con Artist on the Coast

Music Murder Mystery Series

The Sound of Music

West Side Murder

Little Shop of Murder

Once Upon a Murder

Romance in Rehoboth Series (romantic comedy)

Music Man

The Flip

Plot Twist

Badge Bunny

Wedding War

Stage Mom

Shark Bite

Contemporary Romance Standalones

Given to Fly

The Light at Dawn

Reconstructed Heart

Women's Fiction

Fat Girl

Green Castles

Nonfiction

The Fat Girl's Guide to Loving Your Body